The Secrets of
Grindlewood
THE SECRET SCROLL

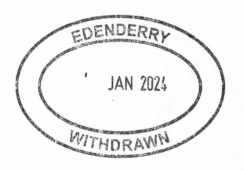

Dedication

For Nora Mathews and Thomas J. Burke,
Mum and Dad

The Secrets of
Grindlewood
THE SECRET SCROLL

JACKIE BURKE

LINDON BOOKS

First published by Lindon Books in 2014,
9 Raheen Park, Bray, Co. Wicklow.
Web: www.grindlewood.com
Email: jackieburke@grindlewood.com

Paperback	ISBN: 978 1 909483 50 7
eBook – mobi format	ISBN: 978 1 909483 51 4
eBook – ePub format	ISBN: 978 1 909483 52 1
CreateSpace edition	ISBN: 978 1 909483 53 8

Produced by Kazoo Independent Publishing Services
222 Beech Park, Lucan, Co. Dublin
www.kazoopublishing.com

Kazoo Independent Publishing Services is not the publisher of this work. All rights and responsibilities pertaining to this work remain with Lindon Books.

Kazoo offers independent authors a full range of publishing services.
For further details visit www.kazoopublishing.com

Cover design by Andrew Brown
Cover and internal illustrations © Fintan Taite 2014
Printed in the EU

About the Author

Jackie grew up with her sister and three brothers in South Dublin. An avid reader and writer since her early school days, she only recently began writing children's stories, having dreamed of doing so for quite some time. *The Secrets of Grindlewood: The Secret Scroll* is the second instalment in the Grindlewood series. Book 1 was released in September 2013.

The series is inspired by all that Jackie loves in nature: gardens, forests, wildlife and especially cats and dogs. Reading, hill walking and baking cakes are just a few of her many hobbies. Jackie lives with her husband in Bray, County Wicklow. They share their home with a big fluffy cat called Millie.

Contents

Chapter One

SECRETS OF GRINDLEWOOD

Two ancient magical clans, the Worfagons and the Wandeleis, had been at war for centuries. Although scattered and unorganised, the remaining Worfagon warlocks seemed to be unstoppable. In contrast, the gentle Wandeleis had no experience of fighting wars, and despite their superior magic, they were slowly being wiped out. It was time for change. Something had to be done.

One day, a brave young witch from the Wandelei clan asked permission from her sad and broken leader, the Forest Queen, to leave the fold and seek out new magic. Wanda knew she needed dark and powerful magic to create complex spells: one, to release her queen from a terrible curse; and a second to destroy the evil warlock Worfeus, leader of the Worfagons. He was intent on continuing the fighting until every last threat to his reign – real or imagined – was eliminated. And that included the Forest Queen, her people and all the residents of Grindlewood.

Hearing of Wanda's personal quest to destroy him, the evil Worfeus decided to go looking for her. He had already destroyed many powerful enemies and he didn't expect much trouble from a young Wandelei witch.

He finally tracked her down near Grindlewood and followed her to her little cottage at the end of an enormous wild garden. There, one fateful day, the witch and the warlock fought a bitter duel, a fight to the death. It was witnessed by a local boy, Luke, who was shocked to see what was happening in Grindlewood garden, a place he often went to play.

Seeing the boy, Worfeus turned to cast a killing spell, but Wanda, in her dying moments, fired a spell of her own to save her little friend. The two spells collided in a massive burst of fireballs and stardust, and the boy disappeared. He was never found.

As Wanda fell slowly into her final sleep, she fired another spell at the sneering, gloating warlock. Thanks to this final curse, Worfeus would become imprisoned in the dark forest behind Grindlewood, once he returned there. And he would be stuck in the form of a wolf. Realising what Wanda had done to him, the warlock was furious. His madness and rage became greater as the months and years passed, fuelling his desire for revenge.

It was five long years before the ever-increasing band of residents of Grindlewood garden even heard of Wanda's quest. They had a visit one night from Oberon, a wise and learned snowy owl. Oberon had once lived near Grindlewood and knew of the duel between Wanda and Worfeus. He told the surprised group of garden friends that it was up to them to stop the wicked warlock now. They must complete Wanda's dangerous quest – a quest to find her secret scroll, cast her super-spell, and destroy the evil warlock before he took his revenge on all of Grindlewood.

The gentle group of garden friends were stunned. They were in grave danger. The owl explained how the evil warlock would stop at nothing to get the scroll and that he would destroy anyone who got in his way, once he escaped the forest. And it wouldn't be long before he figured out how to undo the curse that kept him there.

Bleak and dangerous as the situation seemed, clever Wanda had left many secrets and enchantments behind her to help the residents of Grindlewood continue her quest to destroy the evil warlock for good. As many suspected, she had indeed completed her destroying spell. She had written it on a scroll of parchment and then hidden it safely in the plinth of a fountain that sat in the huge pond in Grindlewood garden. During the coldest winter in years, the pond froze, and the brave group of friends waited anxiously for the spring thaw. Once the ice melted, they planned to recover the scroll and cast the only spell that would rid the world of this most wicked warlock.

While he worked on potions to free himself from Wanda's double curse – imprisoned in the forest and stuck as a wolf – Worfeus created armies of nasty birds and animals to attack Grindlewood garden and bring him news of the residents' search for the secret scroll. So far they hadn't been very successful, but their attacks were nasty and troublesome. Worfeus was a mean and cunning warlock and the residents of Grindlewood had to be braver and smarter than ever before in their lives.

Having recently moved into Grindlewood House, the Grindle family were very excited about their new rambling home and their huge, overgrown garden.

Delighted with their new collection of pets and wildlife, Jamie and Jemima Grindle soon noticed that all was not as it seemed in the garden. They suspected, though, that their beloved pets, Timber the dog and Teddy the cat, were at the very heart of whatever was going on. And indeed they were right.

The pets quickly learned from their new garden friends many of the secrets of Grindlewood's past, and they were eager to join in the quest. It wasn't long before Timber, a brave and loyal dog, stepped forward to lead the animals. He was ready to take on Worfeus. He was determined to finish the quest. He would protect and defend the children, their new home and new friends, from anything.

And so a frantic race was on to reach the secret scroll and finally reveal its super-spell, and any other secrets it might hold, to whoever reached it first.

∾❧∾

Delving into magic and history books, Jamie and Jemima learned a lot about Grindlewood's murky past. Piece by piece, they were beginning to understand just what a special and enchanted place their new home really was. Jemima was a true believer in magic and thought they would find the answers to some extraordinary questions in her growing number of books about Grindlewood, and about magic. Her older brother, Jamie, was a practical boy and he tried to understand what his big dog, Timber, was up to with the other residents of their wild garden. So far neither of the children had come up with many answers that made any sense.

'Not everything can be explained by magic!' said Jamie.

'But it's the only thing that makes sense!' said Jemima.

'Sense! What sense?' asked Jamie.

'Jamie, don't you remember that piece I read from our book about witches and the Forest Queen? You know, the queen who was cursed to grow in the ground like a tree? Oh, that was a terrible curse! Whoever did it must have been very nasty. They must have used very dark magic.'

'I remember,' said Jamie, 'but we don't know if anything in the book is true. All I do know is that Timber is the most fantastic dog in the world – the bravest and cleverest and best dog ever. If he's involved in something that's going on in the garden, something that involves all the animals and birds and everything that lives here, I'd like to know about it. I really need him to talk to me, somehow.'

'Well, how are we going to train the dogs to talk?' asked Jemima. She didn't think Jamie's plan was going to work. 'Look, there are so many mysteries here. Just think about the frog, Ernie. He can heal anything. We've seen him do it. And the butterflies – they told us things about the garden the first day we came here, just by landing in our hair. That's how we knew all the names of the birds and animals!'

'I know,' said Jamie. 'I remember.'

'And what about the Brigadier and Sylvie? We heard that they've belonged to this house for twenty years, but they still look so young. Then there's the fish in the pond. They swim at super-speed and ...' She sighed, and started again, 'I think we can learn more about, well, all those mysteries from these books, especially *The History of Grindlewood* that Mr Finlay gave us, and the twelve volumes of *History of Magic* that Abigail brought over from her granddad's house.'

'I think Grindlewood is pretty amazing too,' said

her brother, 'and I can't explain all that stuff, but I'm going to start lessons with Timber anyway. I'll practise with him every day, and I bet I'll know what he's saying soon enough. Timber and Teddy are friends with the other pets and wildlife now. I think Timber is their leader – how cool is that?' Jamie laughed, then he thought about it some more. 'I don't like the idea that he might be keeping secrets from me, though. He is my dog, after all.'

'Timber would tell you everything if he could,' said Jemima. 'Teddy mightn't though, being a cat. Cats are so secretive. I suppose if we knew what they were talking about, we could probably help them with whatever it is they're doing, somehow, maybe. Hmm.'

'I think Teddy would tell you everything. He adores you. Come on, let's feed Ernie and the goldfish,' said Jamie. Having more or less agreed with each other at last, the two children headed upstairs to Jamie's bedroom.

Before Christmas, they had moved the goldfish and the frog to an indoor home, made especially for them. It was like a miniature pond and rockery in a big glass box, made by the children's father, Greg. It would keep them warm and happy through the winter. They would never be able to survive outside in the freezing cold. Jamie insisted that he take charge of them, so their new winter tank was put in his room. As expected the pond froze hard, and Jamie's new roommates had been taken indoors just in time. There they would stay until the thaw arrived.

Deep in the forest, Worfeus was working hard on his spells and potions right through the winter. The warlock had been stuck there for five years and his patience was running out. He was frantic to get out and go after the secret scroll himself. He would destroy Grindlewood and all who lived there, if they meddled in his plans or prevented him from getting what he wanted – Wanda's scroll. He had eliminated a long line of opponents and there were few left to challenge him. The scroll, and the destroying spell that was written inside it, was the last real threat now that clever Wanda herself was gone.

The angry warlock also wanted a new evil army. He had nearly run out of hags to stir his big, black cauldron. With only two left, he had to consider his choices carefully. He was also down to his last few magpies, a single crow and a rather tattered looking rat. He thought about boiling some or all of them in the pot, and he eyed them menacingly.

Having already brewed up a flock of menacing magpies and cackling crows to do his bidding, he decided he needed something more terrifying this time. So far his evil armies had failed to match the bravery or cleverness of the garden residents. Now Worfeus planned to cook up some truly nasty creatures in his huge bubbling cauldron in the forest. Soon they would be unleashed on the garden.

The Grindlewood birds had been watching Worfeus from their lookout posts for several weeks. They looked on, terrified, as the warlock emerged at the edge of the dark forest. His disgusting green and purple potions were having an awful effect on him. He looked uglier and madder than ever.

Thanks to the purple potion, which he was improving all the time, Worfeus had lengthened the time he could spend in the form of a warlock. Shape-shifting into a wolf was uncomfortable and awkward. But that particular problem was almost at an end.

He hadn't been so successful with his other problem: escaping his forest prison. But by working on his special brew of curdled green gloop, he was slowly able to leave the forest for just a little longer, and go just a little further, every time he tried. He was definitely making progress. The residents of Grindlewood knew this too. Worfeus, the wicked warlock, would soon be able to reach the garden.

Chapter Two

The three foxes, Eldric, Freya and Fern, had agreed to let Norville the hedgehog share their den for the winter. Norville should have been hibernating like other hedgehogs, but it was agreed that they would not hibernate this winter. All the residents of Grindlewood garden would be needed if Worfeus and his evil armies attacked again.

They decided that it would be warmer for all of them if the foxes and hedgehog shared a home through the coldest part of the winter. But it was rather crowded and Norville's spikes were getting on everyone's nerves. One day, there was a terrible row. Freya and Fern were very cross. They wanted Norville out. After all, he had his own little home to go to, even if it was a bit chilly. But for once, Eldric took Norville's side of the argument and the four of them had a big falling out. Freya and Fern stormed off in a huff just as another snow blizzard came down.

After a little while Fern calmed down and returned home.

'So, you've decided to come back?' barked Eldric.

'It's freezing out there, and a terrible snow blizzard has started. I could hardly see where I was going.'

'Well, I'm glad you're back. Did you see Freya?' muttered Eldric.

'No, I lost her in the blizzard,' said Fern, wondering where her sister could have gone.

'Well, while you've been out,' said Norville, 'Eldric and I have been digging out a bit more room at the back.' He pointed to the corner with his nose. 'The ground is very hard, but if we all take turns we might be able to create more space for everyone.' Norville felt guilty that his spikes had caused the row and he was getting worried about Freya. She really should have come back with Fern once the weather had worsened. He looked over at his anxious friend. 'She'll be back soon, Eldric. She'll be getting hungry. You know how she loves her food. Don't worry.'

Freya had started out in such a rage that she hadn't really thought about where she was going. But soon it was snowing very heavily and turning even colder. All this wading and jumping through deep snow was making her very tired and hungry. Her tummy started to rumble. Then she smelled something tempting. 'What is that?' she wondered. 'Hmmm, I think it might be, hmmm, yes, it's, it's … a vole! Yes, it's a vole. Yummy, yummy!' She pressed on through the snow, following her nose.

It was a vole all right – but it was Valerius Vole, Worfeus' devious little servant. He was luring Freya towards the forest, straight into a trap. Worfeus and Valerius had been expecting another visitor from Grindlewood, after Norville's visit a few months earlier. The warlock instructed Valerius to dig a hole in the ground and cover it with dead branches and leaves. Then the vole watched and waited. He was very patient, unlike his master. The warlock had cast a scenting spell to lure any visitors directly to the trap. That scent was now wafting in Freya's direction.

She was so keen to catch something tasty for dinner that she didn't pay enough attention to where she was going. She was thinking of how a surprise feast might make up for her bad temper earlier. But Worfeus and Valerius had other ideas. Their trap was perfect and as Freya eagerly followed her nose, she fell into the cleverly hidden hole. She got a dreadful fright and quickly realised that she was in big trouble.

The unfortunate fox had hurt one of her legs and couldn't jump or climb out of the hole. She tried a few times, but the pain of landing on a wounded leg meant she couldn't do much except wait. Nervously Freya looked up, trying to see what was coming. In a moment, a shape appeared at the top of the ditch – a large, thin, scraggy animal, with small, red-rimmed eyes and a long, thin muzzle that showed sharp teeth. It leaned over the top of the ditch to take a look at its victim. Valerius Vole appeared too, sneering and snivelling. Freya saw them and was terrified.

After some loud growling and wailing, Worfeus struggled out of his wolf shape and back to his true form – the tall, scrawny, evil warlock. Freya looked up horrified, expecting a killing spell. Instead, Worfeus whipped out his wand and began his torture. He cast spell after spell at the wounded fox, cutting and burning her.

'I am Worfeus, Supreme Warlock! Tell me where you're hiding the scroll! I demand to know! Tell me!'

'I don't know, I don't know,' whimpered Freya, trying her best to dodge the burning spells.

Worfeus continued his torture. Eventually, Freya collapsed in a heap, exhausted.

Worfeus stormed back towards his lair to pore over more spell books and potion papers, angrily searching for something that would make the brave little fox tell him what he wanted to know.

'I must find that scroll, I must, I MUST!' he roared to himself. 'Hmm, perhaps I should ask that ragged old buzzard. Yes, yes, he owes me a few favours. He just might have a truly nasty idea or two that would help. Or better still, he might even know something. Hmm, I don't like asking him for too many favours. He might think me weak. Bah! I'll send him a message by magpie!' The angry warlock disappeared into his lair.

Back in the garden, Eldric had told Timber about Freya's disappearance. The blizzard had finally stopped, so the big dog asked the birds to fly around and try to spot her deep rusty coat. Fern and Eldric decided to go beyond the garden to search, but Norville remained in the den. He couldn't move easily in deep snow with such short legs.

Timber told the other pets that Freya was missing. They all knew they were not allowed to leave the garden, but they were getting very agitated doing nothing. Timber spoke to the dogs.

'We can't just sit here and wait,' he said. 'If we make enough noise, the Grindles might come out of the house. We have to make them follow us through the hedge and out into the fields, possibly even as far as the forest. Eldric thinks Freya might have gone in there.'

'Oh dear,' said the Brigadier, 'not that forest.'

'Here goes,' said Dougal, preparing to bark madly. 'Let's hope they don't think we want to play or go for a walk instead.'

Their plan worked. The children ran outside almost immediately, Jamie with his coat half on, half off, and his woolly hat still in his hand.

'What's up, guys? Do you want to play snowballs again?'

Jemima followed quickly, dragging her scarf through the snow. The dogs dashed towards the side of the garden where there was a gap in the hedge. The children followed them.

'Look, Jamie! It's like a little doorway,' said Jemima.

'The dogs want to go through. What is it, Timber?' Jamie asked his dog as he peered through the hedge. He turned and looked very closely at Timber, who was shoving his muzzle through the hedge and digging at the snow.

'Woo-woo-woo,' Timber replied in a low, throaty howl. Jamie looked at Jemima. They were both thinking the same thing. The talking lessons with the dogs were going to be difficult. 'Timber is definitely trying to tell us something, but what?' said Jamie.

'It's so confusing. Almost all the growls sound exactly the same,' said Jemima.

'He wants to go through the hedge,' said Jamie. 'He's digging at the ground right at that gap and sticking his muzzle through. He must want us to go through.'

Then, right in front of them, Eldric and Fern ran around Timber, straight through the hedge and out into the field beyond.

'Where's the other one?' asked Jemima.

'That's it!' said Jamie. 'The third one is missing. What's her name again, Jem?' asked Jamie.

'Freya and Fern, but I'm not sure which is which.

The two smaller foxes look so alike.'

'Right. Let's take the dogs and check this out. Mum and Dad are busy talking to Mr and Mrs Diggle. They won't even notice we're gone.'

'I know – they didn't even see us leave the room,' said Jemima.

'Will you go to the barn and grab the old walking stick, just in case,' said Jamie, still looking at Timber, trying to understand all his little growls.

'In case of what?' asked Jemima.

'I don't know, just in case. We might have to go as far as the forest, and who knows what's in there,' replied Jamie a little uncomfortably. 'Remember what Mr Finlay told Dad? He said that the forest is dark and dangerous.'

'I remember,' said Jemima. 'When Luke disappeared, they thought he might have got lost in the forest.' Timber growled. He didn't like the idea of the children going into the forest.

'I know, it might be scary, but if one of the animals is lost or hurt, we have to rescue it, don't we?'

Jemima thought for a moment. 'Jamie, do you think Luke might have found something in the forest, maybe even some magic, and that he got into trouble?'

'It's possible, I suppose,' said Jamie. 'Who knows? Come on, we should get going.'

The dogs were very anxious. They had hoped to get the children's parents' attention, but now the children were getting ready to go out into the field with them. All three of them were barking and Dougal was scratching at the hedge. Jamie hadn't seen them so wound-up before. Once Jemima returned from the barn, they all squeezed through the gap in the hedge. They tramped across the big back field that led to the forest, jumping and kicking their way through the thick blanket of snow. The dogs surged forward, their noses working hard to pick up Freya's scent.

'I was right, Jem. We are heading for the forest,' said Jamie.

'Look, I can see red fur. There, straight ahead,' cried Jemima.

Eldric was just ahead of them. He had suspected trouble once he saw fox paw prints in the snow leading straight to the forest. As they got closer, the three dogs stopped barking and just growled as they sensed the danger ahead. The blackbirds had perched in trees just outside the forest. They were too scared to go in.

'The foxes might have found the missing one already.'

'Oh, I hope she's all right,' said Jemima.

They plodded on through the snow as quickly as they could. As they got closer, they could hear Freya's cries getting louder, piercing the otherwise silent surroundings.

'Listen to that. She must be injured,' said Jemima.

'Come on, we'd better hurry,' urged Jamie.

Timber bounded ahead towards Eldric and Fern. He greeted them with a sniff and a lick.

'She's in there,' said Eldric, looking very worried.

'Don't worry,' said Timber. 'We'll get her out, and Ernie will heal her as soon as we get her home.'

'But how will we get her out?' whimpered Fern.

'Look,' said Timber as Jamie and Jemima arrived with Dougal and the Brigadier. The foxes stood beside the dogs, sniffing and growling. The children watched. They knew the animals were talking.

'Timber, lead us to the fox. Good boy, find the fox,' said Jamie, knowing his dog would obey. Timber gave his obedience growl and they entered the forest all together, Timber in the lead.

This forest wasn't like any they had ever seen before. Despite all the snow, it was dark and dreary. Although trees would naturally sleep through the winter, these trees looked dead. It was a very cold day in the middle of winter but the temperature fell further in the forest, and became colder still the further in they went.

Gnarled and exposed roots from dead trees were everywhere, along with dead twigs, broken branches and rotten tree stumps. The children had to walk carefully through all the debris. Thick, clingy ivy vines wove through the broken twigs and roots, making the forest floor more like an obstacle course. A stinking fog lingered at the edge of the forest too, and the stench grew stronger as they started to move towards the centre.

'Whew! What is that pong?' cried Jamie.

'It's disgusting,' said Jemima, wrinkling up her nose. 'I hope we won't be long in here. It's the creepiest place I've ever seen – and smelled. Urgh!'

'Me too, ugh!' said Jamie, lifting one gloved hand to his nose to try to block the smell. The dogs and foxes smelled the foul air too but their noses were trying hard to find Freya and that kept them busy.

Luckily, it wasn't long before they reached the injured fox. Timber stopped at the edge of the hole and growled to warn the others not to fall in.

'Oh no, she's hurt! Look at her leg and she has weird marks all over her, look!' cried Jamie, crouching down. 'How did that happen?'

'They look like burns,' said Jemima.

'Burns!' said Jamie, 'What could do that out here, in the cold and the snow?'

'I wonder *who* did it,' said Jemima. 'Maybe it was fireworks,' she said, thinking about it a bit more.

'I didn't see or hear any, did you?' said Jamie, looking carefully at the fox.

'Well if it wasn't fireworks, it could have been dark magic, Jamie, really bad stuff,' whispered Jemima.

Jamie jumped down into the hole and carefully lifted the fox into his arms.

'Timber, is this Fern?' asked Jamie, looking up at his dog. The two smaller foxes looked so alike it was hard to tell which was which. Eldric, being the male fox, was bigger, so he was easy to recognise.

Timber growled.

'I guess not,' said Jemima. 'It must be Freya then.'

Timber barked and wagged his tail.

'It's Freya,' said both children together.

The three dogs growled and Timber pawed uneasily at the ground.

'I think it's time to go,' said Jamie. 'It's all right, Freya. We'll take you back to Ernie. He'll fix you up,' he said to the fox. He placed her gently out of the hole before climbing out himself. The children heard some shuffling in the bushes behind them, but glancing around, they saw nothing. They could sense that someone or something was watching them. They were scared now. The dogs growled louder. They too sensed danger. The foxes were still sniffing Freya to see if she was OK.

Jemima looked nervously around. Thick tubes of fog had emerged from behind a clump of dead trees. They wound their way along the ground, curling around the children's feet and the animals' paws, like snakes slithering through a soupy river.

They all felt a deep shiver and chill, except Timber, who was howling like a wolf. The other two dogs were barking and growling. All three of them were pawing at the ground, sniffing and strutting about. They were very uneasy, and at the same time, they seemed ready for a fight. It was definitely time to leave such a creepy, miserable place.

The warlock's servant, Valerius Vole, had been watching them, but there was little he could do to stop them rescuing the fox. He ran off to report back to Worfeus.

Jamie carried Freya in his arms as they all walked back to the garden. Timber led the group from the front again, howling all the way home. The dogs and foxes hopped and jumped along beside them through the snow.

Their neighbours, the Diggles, had already left, so the children's parents, Greg and Gloria, were in the garden calling for them. As the whole group crawled through the hedge with the injured fox, their parents were standing in front of them.

'Oh! Mum, Dad, this fox has hurt her leg, but I think she'll be OK,' said Jamie, hoping to get the injured animal to the healing frog as quickly as possible. He also wanted to avoid awkward questions of where and how it had happened. No chance.

'What? Where did you find her?' asked Gloria.

'Um, she was, um, just outside the hedge, sort of, in a hole. We heard her yelping and um, I think she has a broken leg,' muttered Jamie.

'Those look like burns. How did that happen?' said Greg as he looked closely at the injured animal. 'Bring her inside, quickly. I hope you two weren't messing with fireworks.'

'No way, Dad. Honestly, we didn't do this. We found her. We were just trying to help,' said Jamie, feeling rather offended. They all went into the kitchen.

The dogs and foxes stood together at the open kitchen door, watching. The three cats trotted into the kitchen to take a look. Jamie placed the fox on the floor. Jemima had left the kitchen, but returned quickly, half drenched.

'Jemima, what on earth were you doing?' asked Gloria.

'Mum, I had to get the frog. He can heal the fox, really he can.'

'What?' cried Gloria, looking at Greg, who shrugged his shoulders. Neither of them knew what their daughter was talking about, but the children had seen the frog's magical ability before.

Jemima carefully placed Ernie on the floor beside Freya. He had been sleeping peacefully in his tank, when Jemima burst in and whipped him out. He looked at the fox with a start. He quickly hopped about and kissed all of Freya's wounds. In a few moments she was healed. She raised her head slowly off the floor, and looked around. She gave a few gentle barks and stood up.

'Well, well, well!' said Greg.

'Oh, look, she's fine!' said Gloria.

The children cheered and the animals barked and meowed, making quite a racket.

'You see, I told you the frog could do it!' cried Jemima.

'Hurray for Ernie!' shouted Jamie, and he quickly picked up the frog before he got stood on in all the excitement. He popped Ernie back in his tank with some extra food as a reward. The foxes ran out of the kitchen and back to their den where a very cheerful Norville was shivering at the entrance.

'Well, Gloria, that frog must be an extraordinary breed. Unless, of course, the fox wasn't really injured at all,' said Greg, scratching his head.

'Hmm,' said Gloria. 'Don't some animals have unusual healing powers?'

'Yes, that could be it. I'm sure I heard of something like that on one of those nature programmes Jamie likes to watch. I wouldn't have thought a simple pond frog could do that, though,' said Greg.

'Well, maybe he's not an ordinary pond frog,' whispered Gloria mischievously. 'He might even be worth a fortune!' She laughed and went to put the kettle on.

The children were talking outside.

'Jamie, did you notice, in the forest, you know?' asked Jemima.

'Well, it was cold, dark and creepy. What else?' asked Jamie.

'I had the strangest feeling in there. It's such a weird place,' said Jemima. 'I think we are very close to magic, Jamie, maybe dark magic. It's a bit scary, but it's exciting too!'

Her brother looked at her as if she might be a bit crazy.

'Come on, Jemima, a little bit of magic I can take. Stuff like Ernie the frog and his healing ability. But what is *dark* magic, anyway?'

'It's bad magic, Jamie – evil magic – though sometimes even good magic needs to be mixed with dark magic to be powerful enough for certain spells to work, according to Abigail's books, anyway.'

Jamie looked confused, but Jemima continued.

'And if there is dark magic around here, someone has to stop it, or it will destroy everything.'

'What?' cried Jamie. 'You can't be serious!'

'I've read it in my books, Jamie. I'll show you the chapters later. There is definitely something weird and spooky – and important – about that forest,' said Jemima, wringing her hands. She always did that when she was excited and talking at the same time. 'And if there is something going on in there, we really should do something about it. Who else will take care of it?'

'Well, we could take another look, I suppose,' muttered Jamie. He was thinking more of how he loved exploring forests than about finding trouble or dark magic. They would take Timber with them, of course, just in case.

'OK, but it'll have to be just a quick look, or we'll get into serious trouble, and not just with any of that dark magic, Jemima. Mum and Dad will go mental!'

Chapter Three

DANGER IN THE FOREST

It was Saturday afternoon. All the pets were inside by the fire except Timber, who liked to be outside. He never minded the cold. He was patrolling the garden, barking now and again, checking everything was in order. Jamie and Jemima wrapped up warmly and went outside. They played with Timber for a little while, but they were really waiting for their chance to sneak away.

'OK, are we ready?' asked Jamie.

'Ready,' replied Jemima.

They looked at each other. They were excited about going to the forest again, but also a little uncomfortable. It was a very strange place, but their curiosity was too great. They simply had to return. They wondered, too, if whatever it was that Timber and the rest of the garden residents were up to might in some way be linked to the forest. The animals seemed to be very interested in the forest, and Freya had wandered in there alone. Jamie wondered about that.

Jemima had read passages in her books that mentioned a forest again and again – but was it their forest? And if so, what was so special about it?

Jamie called Timber to the gap in the hedge. 'Come on, Timber, you're coming with us,' he said.

His dog looked at him. He growled and sat in an upright positon. He didn't think they should go.

'Come on, Timber, we're going back to the forest. Come on, boy,' said Jamie.

Timber stood up, gave a reluctant woof and sat down again.

Jamie tugged on his collar. 'Come on, Timber, walkies.'

Timber didn't like it but he knew he had to obey. He couldn't let the children go alone. So off the three of them went, through the hedge once again, heading straight for the forest.

The robins were in the garden and they spotted them leaving. They were very concerned. They sat on the kitchen windowsill and pecked at the window, trying to get the attention of one of the cats.

'What is it?' asked Sylvie, shaking herself awake.

'The children have taken Timber out through the hedge,' said Reggie Robin. 'We think they're going to the forest again.'

'Oh, no!' said Teddy. 'What are they doing?'

'We don't know, but what could Timber do?' said Ruby. 'Jamie called him and told him he had to go with them.'

'You're right, they are heading for the forest,' said Binky Blackbird, returning from a quick fly-over. 'Where's their mum?'

'She's gone out,' said Sylvie.

'Whatever is the matter?' asked the Brigadier, joining them from his snooze by the fire. He was quickly followed by Dougal, shaking his floppy ears to wake up.

'The children left the garden through the hedge. The robins saw them. They took Timber,' said Sylvie quickly.

'Oh dear, oh no!' said the Brigadier. 'We must do something.'

'Their parents are out,' said Teddy.

'We'll have to go after the children and Timber right away,' said Dougal.

'How can you get out? You're too big for the cat flap,' said Cindy.

'I can open the back door by jumping at the handle and knocking it down so that the door opens,' said Dougal excitedly. The cats looked at him, surprised. They hadn't realised that the spaniel was that clever.

'Really, I can,' said Dougal. 'Come on, Brigadier.'

Dougal raced over to the door that opened to the back yard. He crouched low then leapt up at the handle, knocking it down just enough to open the door.

'Well, well, that's a neat trick!' said the Brigadier.

'Thanks!' said Dougal.

'Let's go,' said the Brigadier. 'Hey, wait a minute – we can't go after them. We're not allowed to leave the garden. Anyway, it has always been my job to give the orders, ahem, ahem.'

'I know, sorry, but this is an emergency, isn't it?' said Dougal. 'I mean, Worfeus is out there. Jamie and Jemima could get into serious trouble. What else can we do?'

'Yes, we may need human help this time,' said Teddy. 'Now I understand why Timber's putting up with those talking lessons. They just might be useful some day – and soon. Come on, Sylvie, Cindy, we'll wait for Gloria and lead her outside when she gets home. She'll be able to see your paw prints in the snow, Brigadier, and then she'll follow you to the children.'

'Good thinking, Teddy,' said the Brigadier.

The cats ran to the front of the house to watch for Gloria. The two dogs ran out the back door, into the garden and down to the gap in the hedge.

The children had felt quite excited walking across the field with Timber, but once they reached the forest they felt differently. The cold, damp and dark seemed to stick to them. The clouds gathered and darkened overhead and sank down so close that the children thought they could nearly touch them if they jumped. They shuddered with the chill and stumbled over the many lumpy, twisted roots protruding all over the forest floor. The roots seemed much thicker and more twisted than the day before, and perhaps there were even more of them. It was very creepy. Timber was sniffing around nearby, growling softly. He wasn't happy about being in the forest at all and hoped they wouldn't be staying long.

'Just think what we might find, Jamie,' said Jemima,

trying to feel excited about being there. 'They say the oldest magic began in the forests, and that's why wands come from the oldest forest trees.'

'Really?' said Jamie. 'These trees look pretty dead. Surely you wouldn't get a decent wand from any of them.'

'It's weird. I mean, I know the trees go to sleep in the winter, but these look odd,' said Jemima.

'Long dead,' said Jamie.

They passed the animal trap where Freya had been caught.

'I wonder what they were hoping to catch,' said Jamie. 'Surely not a fox.' That thought made both the children more nervous. What was the trap really for?

As they moved deeper into the forest, they heard strange hissing and bubbling noises. There were more disgusting smells wafting their way too. They were putrid, horrid smells and Jemima started to feel sick. A few twigs cracked close by. 'Maybe this wasn't such a good idea after all,' thought Jamie. 'I'll be blamed if anything goes wrong, just because I'm the oldest. I hope this hasn't been a giant mistake.'

Jamie's head was spinning as he looked slowly around and about, trying to spot danger before it pounced on them. There was definitely something extra creepy about this forest. It wasn't at all normal. Fog was curling around their feet and ankles again. It seemed to come from out of nowhere. The further in they went, the thicker the fog became and the higher it snaked around them. It was getting colder and darker too.

There was a sharp crack ahead of them. The two children stood still. They heard nothing else, but the fog seemed to change shape. It swirled and closed in on them, like a monster chasing after its prey.

'Oh Jamie, this fog is horrible. It looks like it's going to swallow us,' whispered Jemima, lifting her head, as the swirls of fog thickened and rose as high as her neck.

'Uh oh,' Jamie croaked back.

'What?' asked Jemima, in a tiny whisper.

'I think we've found trouble.'

'Did you hear something?'

'No, I thought I saw something.'

'What?'

'Eyes – over there, staring at us.'

'What? Where? I can't see any,' said Jemima, trying to see through the soupy fog.

'Over there,' said Jamie, pointing. The fog was so thick just then that neither of the children could even see Jamie's outstretched hand.

'What'll we do? Oh, it's so hard to see,' said Jemima.

'Stop right here,' said Jamie. 'There's something out there. Where's Timber?'

'Uh oh,' gasped Jemima.

The children stood absolutely still. They could hear Timber growling but he was hidden by the fog. Jamie took a deep breath and leapt out in front of his sister, brandishing the walking stick as if it were a sword.

'Get back, go away, ahhhhh!' Jamie roared at whatever it was, hoping to scare it off.

'Run, Jemima, run!' he yelled, but Jemima froze.

Through the shifting, swirling fog, Jamie could just make out two red-rimmed yellow eyes above a snarling muzzle. The large, mangy wolf pawed angrily at the ground, then started its approach. It crouched low, stalking steadily around the withered trees and bushes, never taking his eyes off them, or so it seemed.

But it wasn't Jamie and Jemima he was after, not yet. Something else posed a bigger threat. There was more snarling and growling coming from behind the two children. Stuck to the spot and absolutely terrified, Jemima felt warm breath on her left ear and then something big and furry brushed past her.

The wolf was not in the least bothered by Jamie's shouting or his stick. The animal was closing in. He leapt up and swiped a long thin paw at Jamie's face, knocking him out of the way. Jamie fell on a clump of knotted tree roots that bruised his right arm, bumped his head, and he had a nasty cut on his cheek from the wolf's claws. Jamie was stunned for a moment and didn't move. Jemima tried to scream but nothing would come out of her mouth.

Something else came around from behind the children. Jemima finally gave a weak cry and stumbled sideways as she tried to turn and run. Jamie started to shout and then tried to stand up, but he fell down again. Something was gripping his ankles and dragging him behind the old tree. He struggled to free himself but his ankles were quickly tied up. He tried to inch himself away from the tree and the crawling roots, as well as what was in front of him – two large animals preparing to fight.

Suddenly Timber and the wolf leapt out and crashed together mid-air. The children weren't the warlock's target. It was Timber who had caught

Worfeus' eye as the brave dog brushed past Jemima, ready to defend the two children. The malamute and the wolf tore at each other, biting savagely. Loud barks, growls and snarls filled the air. They rolled over on the ground, each one trying to gain the upper hand. Dust, twigs and fur flew about as the animals fought. It was ferocious. Blood quickly streamed from both animals, but the wicked wolf seemed to have the edge. He was bigger than Timber and a lot meaner. But Timber battled bravely on. He would never give up.

Jemima finally found her voice and screamed the most piercing scream. It echoed right through the forest, even startling the menacing magpies around the cauldron.

Jamie was still struggling with the tree roots that had wound around his feet and ankles, and now some ivy vines were also creeping over his shoulders after they had swung down from overhead branches. They were too strong for him to rip or pull away.

'Jamie, use your knife, the pocket knife!' yelled Jemima, as she ran towards him.

'Aaahh!' was all Jamie could say as he tried to free himself. The vines were now growing around one of his wrists as well. Finally he managed to get his other hand into his pocket and he pulled out a small, sharp pocket knife. He had to work quickly, cutting the vines and roots that had ensnared him. They started to grow back almost as fast as he cut them open. Working quickly, Jemima helped pull the cut pieces away, and once Jamie was freed, they ran away from the creepers as fast as they could, all the time trying to see if Timber was OK.

The dog was still in the middle of a terrible fight. The children had to help him, but all they had was Jamie's small scout's knife.

They heard barking. Dougal and the Brigadier arrived and jumped straight into the action. The three dogs battled against the vicious wolf – the warlock, Worfeus. Poor Timber had fought so much already he was covered in bites. Dougal and the Brigadier were smaller dogs, but they tried their best to help their friend overcome the wolf.

Jamie stepped forward, breathing deeply, holding the knife in one hand and the walking stick in the other. He had to help his pets. Even though there were three dogs against him, the wolf had extraordinary strength.

'I have to help,' said Jamie, as Jemima realised what

he was going to do. Before she could say a word, Jamie jumped in. He tried to beat the wolf back with the stick, but this didn't really help. He had to get closer. It was extremely dangerous. With the dogs jumping and rolling around so much, Jamie had to be careful that he didn't stab one of them by mistake. Once or twice, the wolf snapped viciously in Jamie's direction, but most of his attention was on Timber. The big dog was his main concern.

Finally Jamie got his chance and, lunging forward, he stabbed the wolf. Worfeus howled loudly and Jamie jumped back, quite shocked by what he had done. Dougal and the Brigadier retreated too, injured and exhausted. Timber was lying on the ground.

Worfeus, the wolf, the warlock, whimpered. Blood ran from the back of his neck. He stood still, pricking his ears up as if listening. No one else heard a thing. Everyone stared at Timber. He wasn't moving. The wolf snarled at the children and the dogs, and then he turned and ran off to his lair. The danger seemed to have passed, but Timber still didn't move.

The children knelt beside their dog. He was lying on his side, bleeding and shaking. Dougal and the Brigadier had also been hurt but they didn't look as bad as Timber. He had taken the most terrible mauling. The children looked at their beloved dog and both of them burst into tears. They thought he was dead.

Dougal barked hoarsly. The children looked around and then up at the swooshing noise of large wings. It was Cyril, the heron from Grindlewood's pond. He was carrying something in his mouth. He landed gracefully and dropped his package gently on the ground.

'Good grief!' said the heron, 'What happened? The blackbirds said you were here. Then I heard all the terrible barking and knew there was trouble, but you three look awful! Oh, my, is Timber all right?' He went over to look. He peered up at the children's sad faces. His own face showed how worried he was. The dogs quickly explained everything.

'Don't worry, look who I brought with me!' said Cyril. 'I thought he might be needed.'

'Ernie, Ernie!' screamed Jemima. Jamie grabbed the well-squashed and bumped-about frog and placed him on Timber's side.

'Fix him, Ernie, fix him! Please, please! cried Jemima.

'Go on, Ernie, please,' begged Jamie.

Jamie held Timber's head in his hands, tears streaming down his face. Everyone looked on, hoping their funny, warty frog would be able to save the big brave dog.

Ernie was horrified by Timber's awful injuries. They were the worst he had ever seen. He hopped all over him, kissing the cuts and wounds and bites one by one, tears falling from his bulging eyes. He even started kissing them a second time just to be sure.

They all watched and waited. It seemed to be taking a bit longer than usual. The waiting was awful. Ernie hopped over to Dougal and the Brigadier and healed all their injuries. And still everyone waited. Finally Timber stirred and then sat up. He lifted his head and gave Ernie a generous lick. He looked around to see if everyone was all right and then stood up and shook himself. He howled a terrific big howl to let them all know he was fine. Timber the Super-mal was a hero once again, but more importantly, he was alive and well. The children hugged and kissed him.

It was time to return home. Cyril took off with Ernie sitting uncomfortably in his huge beak, as the others walked out of the forest.

Once outside, they heard the most terrifying rant. It seemed to come from deep in the forest, out of the fog, which was swirling thickly again.

'So, you think you can get the better of me, do you? I, Worfeus, Supreme Warlock of Grindlewood will take what is mine and destroy what I don't want – which is most of this wretched place. Mark my words. Mark my WARNING!' the warlock bellowed. 'I will destroy all of Grindlewood. I will kill the animals and curse the humans, just like my ancestors cursed that stupid Forest Queen! BAH!'

The children didn't stop to look back, but hurried on as fast as they could. Luckily, whoever or whatever it was didn't follow them.

'Yikes! Who was that?' said Jamie.

'Let's get out of here,' said Jemima. 'There's dark magic all over this forest.'

Jamie was hobbling after being badly cut around the ankles by the crawling roots and vines. They stopped to take a look at his injuries.

'Jamie, your right ankle is a real mess,' said Jemima.

'I know. It really hurts,' said Jamie, wincing in pain.

Timber sniffed around Jamie's ankle. He stood back, and let out an enormous howl. In a moment, Cyril returned with Ernie.

'What is it?' asked Cyril.

'I think Jamie needs some of Ernie's magic,' said Timber.

'Oh, yes, I see. But will it work on humans?'

'I don't know, Cyril, but let's give it a try. OK, Ernie?'

'OK with me,' replied the frog.

Jamie and Jemima couldn't understand the animals' conversation, but it was pretty clear what they were up to. They had never thought they might need Ernie's powers. Jamie sat down in the snow and Ernie hopped onto his leg. He kissed all the sore wounds on his ankle and then hopped up his arm, onto his shoulder and kissed the deep scratch on his face and the bump on his head.

'Ow! Ow! That's really sore! Ow!' yelled Jamie.

'Uh oh, maybe the frog can't heal people,' said Jemima, worried that it might have been a mistake to try.

'So long as it doesn't get worse,' cried Jamie. He winced again. His eyes were watering and he looked extremely pale. Suddenly, messing with magic didn't seem like a very good idea at all.

They all waited anxiously for a few moments. The dogs curled up close to Jamie to keep him warm. Ernie was so worried he kissed all the wounds again. Jamie didn't cry out this time. He didn't say anything at all. Jemima was very worried.

'Aaahh!' roared Jamie, sitting up suddenly. 'Oh, that was awful!'

'Look, you're healed!' squealed Jemima.

The dogs barked and Cyril flapped his huge wings. Ernie bounced around on Jamie's lap in celebration. In a few minutes Jamie was able to stand up. He still had a scar on his face and ankles, but that didn't matter.

'I don't mind scars, Jem. They're badges of bravery,' said Jamie, with a big grin. He was feeling a bit like a hero now, just like Timber. 'Thank you very much, Ernie. You really are a wonder-frog!'

Ernie was delighted.

It was definitely time to head home. Jemima was dying to tell her friend Abigail everything that had happened and see if any of their books could explain the dark and creepy forest, the wolf and especially the ranting warlock.

❧

It had been over five years since Luke had disappeared and his father, Arthur Finlay, still believed that the dark forest behind Grindlewood had somehow taken his son away. Five years ago it was a normal forest, with lovely trees and ferns flourishing like any woodland setting. No one was sure that Luke had gone into the forest the day he disappeared, but despite a long search, the boy was never found. Now that Jamie and Jemima were missing, their parents were worried.

The cats had leapt all over her as soon as Gloria came into the house. She knew that meant trouble. She had checked the house and garden but there was no sign of the children. Then she tried some of their friends but no one had heard from them.

'Don't worry, Gloria. We'll find them. Timber would never let anything happen to them,' said Greg.

'I know, but it's so unlike them to wander off like that, especially after we told them not to,' said Gloria.

Having spotted all the footprints near the gap in the hedge, Greg and Gloria decided to head out to the field to take a look. They had just squeezed through the hedge when they saw the two children and the dogs tramping through the snow on their way back home. The children would have a lot of explaining to do.

After supper the family gathered for a serious conversation.

'But Mum, Dad, we just wanted to explore,

that's all,' said Jamie, feebly. They didn't really have an excuse for going off like that, not one they were willing to share.

'Jamie, I think it is abundantly clear that there could have been a great tragedy today,' said Greg sternly.

'You mean if Ernie the frog didn't have magical healing powers?' said Jemima.

'No, I mean if you hadn't been very, very lucky,' said her father.

'But it was Ernie who healed Timber,' said Jemima.

'Timber wouldn't have needed healing if he hadn't been protecting you two from a wolf,' said Greg, sounding more and more cross.

'Timber would've beaten that wolf, I know he would,' said Jamie.

'That's not the point. You could have been killed,' said Gloria, 'and Timber could have died trying to save you.'

'Ernie can heal anything. He's got magic, Dad,' said Jemima.

'We were just trying to find out what's going on around here. The animals seem to know something about that forest,' Jamie blurted out. The thought of Timber dying while trying to save him was really upsetting him.

'I don't want to hear any more excuses,' said Greg. 'As for the frog, well, he must be some quirk of nature. There must be something in his mouth that can heal wounds. I don't know. It doesn't matter. Promise us right now, that you will not wander off on your own again.'

'OK, Dad,' muttered Jamie.

'Yes, Dad,' said Jemima in a whisper.

'Is that a scratch on your face, Jamie? And I don't know what to make of your clothes. They're ruined,' said Gloria.

'That scratch, eh, I don't really remember.'

'And the trousers?' said Gloria.

'Climbing trees again?' asked Greg.

'Um, yeah, trees, sort of,' muttered Jamie.

'All right, then, we can find new trousers,' said Greg. 'Come on, we'll leave it at that.'

Greg and Gloria left the room. The children were feeling confused and upset.

'Maybe we shouldn't have gone,' said Jemima weakly.

'WHAT!' shrieked Jamie. 'You wanted to find magic and dark stuff – whatever you call it. You said the forest was full of magic! Oh, what was I thinking?

We should have just stuck to the dog-talking lessons. At least they wouldn't get any of us killed!'

'I know, I know,' said Jemima, feeling just as guilty as her brother. 'I'm sorry, Jamie, but I really do think there is magic around here. My books say that …'

'I don't care about the books right now. All I can think of is that we nearly got Timber killed, and all because we were looking for magic or whatever it is that the animals are up to.' Jamie was really more upset than angry, and as usual he calmed down quickly. 'Oh, this is crazy. I don't know what to think.'

'Jamie, there has to be magic at work here, there just has to be,' said Jemima. 'Think about Ernie. And what about the butterflies and how they told us all the animals' names, and the pets having meetings at night? They know something, Jamie, and anyway, we were just trying to help. I still think we should help.'

'I know, but let's not put any of our pets in danger again, OK? I couldn't bear it if anything ever happened to Timber, or any of them.' Jamie paused for a moment. There was something else they needed to talk about. 'What about that crazy guy who was roaring at us? What was that about?'

'I don't know. He sounded completely mad,' said Jemima. 'And he said he was a warlock.'

'Maybe he's just some nutter who thinks he's a warlock. Maybe …'

'But what if he is a real warlock? That would mean he knows magic,' said Jemima, 'dark magic.'

'I don't know,' said Jamie. 'I don't know what to think.'

'Well, if he is a warlock, there's bound to be a mention of him somewhere in one of the books.'

'I guess so,' said Jamie.

'Should we tell Mum and Dad about him?' asked Jemima.

'Hmm, a warlock is kind of hard to explain, isn't it? We need to be sure, and anyway, we're in enough trouble already. Let's wait a bit.'

'You're right. Grown-ups don't really like hearing about magic stuff, do they? I'll see if I can find anything that might help us explain it,' said Jemima.

Neither of them liked the idea of telling their parents about a mad warlock, not after they had already tried to explain about the frog's magic. That was easier to explain but it hadn't gone down very well at all.

Jamie went out to feed the pets. Jemima returned to her books, but she found it very hard to read. The extraordinary events of the day were buzzing around in both their heads. The children were more puzzled than ever.

Chapter Four

SPRING THAW

'Jamie, I've been thinking about the mad guy, the warlock. It's strange that he roared like that but didn't come after us. I mean, he sounded really angry and yet he didn't do anything.'

'I know, and I'm glad! I think that wolf must belong to him, though. He was really wild, just like his mad owner,' said Jamie.

'I wonder …' muttered Jemima.

'What's the difference between a wizard and a warlock?' asked Jamie.

'I've been trying to figure that out for ages,' said Jemima. She opened a large book. 'Here, *The History of Magic* says:'

Warlocks often dabble in dark magic and are particularly cunning and devious. They rarely have friends and often live alone in secluded places.

'I guess wizards can be nice or nasty, then, unlike warlocks. Which means what we saw in the forest must be – a bad guy. He certainly sounded horrible, not to mention all the dark magic he used: the vines, the roots, the wolf, the fog, oh, and the smell, ugh!' she said, closing the book. 'He must have done all of that.'

'Sounds like it,' said Jamie. 'And I don't like him being so close, and Timber being attacked like that.'

They heard the doorbell and knew it must be their friend Abigail. They were both looking forward to her visit.

Abigail was really interested in magic. They could talk to her about all this crazy stuff, even if they felt they had to keep it a secret from grown-ups. And they had so much to tell her and so many books, the three of them had plenty of do! Strangely, no one seemed to be able to get to the end of the biggest book, *The History of Grindlewood*. It was truly enormous. While they were reading, Jamie suddenly had a wild idea.

'Yikes!' cried Jamie.

'What is it?' asked Jemima.

'I think I know why we can't finish that big book, the history one.'

'Why?' asked Abigail. Jamie looked startled and was staring at the book very oddly.

'What is it, Jamie?' said Jemima.

'I think it grows,' he said, still staring at the book.

'What! Don't be silly. It can't …' Jemima turned towards the book and looked closely. Jamie still hadn't taken his eyes off it. Abigail followed their stares.

'He's right!' cried Abigail. 'It's definitely thicker than before. Look!'

The three of them went over to the book and turned the pages.

'Go to the back,' said Abigail. Jemima quickly turned more pages.

'Oh, wow!' said Jamie.

'It's bigger, it's longer, it's …' Jemima stuttered.

'It's updating itself!' cried Abigail.

'Wow, oh, wow!' said Jamie. 'It's got the bit about us in the forest, and the warlock. Look!' They all took a look and Jemima read out a little passage. They needed to hear it, as well as see it, to believe it.

The boy was ensnared by the vines of poison ivy, and the cursed tree roots also enjoyed their hold on him. They would have dragged him to the warlock's lair if he and his sister had not been clever enough to escape their evil clutches.

'This is unbelievable,' said Jamie.

'This is real magic,' said Abigail. Jemima read on.

All the while, Worfeus, in the form of a wolf, struggled to defeat the brave and loyal malamute, Timber. He would forever be remembered as a defender of the good. The dog feared nothing and would fight to the death to protect the children. Their encounter was interrupted by a messenger, who called the warlock back to his lair for important news.

'What? Read that again!' said Jamie.

They all read the last bit again. They didn't understand how the warlock was called back to his lair.

'I thought I stabbed him and he ran off!' cried Jamie, a little upset that he wasn't given credit for defeating the wolf.

'Jamie, this means you really stabbed a warlock. Not many people would have dared to do that,' said Abigail.

Jamie felt quite chuffed. He hadn't thought of it like that.

'That's right,' said Jemima. 'But we didn't hear any messenger call the warlock away. So what does that bit mean?'

'Well, we don't know what kind of signal was used,' said Abigail.

'Signal, or magic,' said Jemima.

Abigail nodded.

'This is getting weirder and weirder,' said Jamie.

'I wonder what else will appear in it,' said Abigail. 'There could be more stuff added, maybe even every day.' That was a very exciting thought.

When it was time for Abigail to go home, the history book was put carefully back on the shelf. Jemima's bedroom was beginning to look just like a library, but she didn't mind. She loved her books, and this one was certainly special. It was going to be hard to sleep, watching to see if the big book got any bigger!

With the approach of spring, thoughts soon turned to the awakening wildlife, birds nesting, trees budding and ice melting. The children had noticed that the ducks had left the pond in the winter and hadn't returned.

'I wonder why they all left,' said Jemima, at the breakfast table one morning.

'The pond is frozen, Jem,' said Jamie.

'I know, but maybe they were just too scared after all the rats. Or maybe they know something we don't,' said Jemima in a whisper.

Jamie gave her that look that said, 'Don't say anything in front of Mum and Dad.'

'Perhaps I could build a shelter, a little duck house. If the ducks like it, they might come back,' said Greg, looking over his newspaper. It wasn't the answer the children were looking for, but it sounded like a fun idea.

'Cool, Dad, more building,' said Jamie. 'Can I help you this time?'

'I don't see why not,' said Greg, glad to have found a distraction after all the recent troubles. He felt he had been a bit hard on them over the forest incident.

One weekend towards the end of February, the

new duck house was ready. Just enough ice had melted at the shallow end of the pond so that Greg could cross in waterproof waders to the reedy mound. The duck house was up in no time.

'The ducks are bound to return soon, now that they have a nice new home,' said Greg, shivering as he climbed out of the pond. It was still frightfully cold.

'I hope so,' said Jemima. After all they had discovered recently, she wasn't so sure.

'Don't worry. I'm sure the ducks will spot the new house when they fly overhead,' said her father. In fact, the wood pigeons had already left the garden to give the ducks the good news.

The garden really came alive when the ice finally thawed after more than two and a half long months. Ernie and the goldfish were popped back into the pond, and Cyril, the heron, returned to his perch on the statue. Everyone in the garden was both excited and nervous: it was time to find out if the secret scroll was really in the bottom of the fountain.

It was very dark in the deeper part of the pond. The base of the plinth was covered in quite a lot of mud and grime, making it difficult to see anything. Ernie and the goldfish tried many times to find a little door or a little lock, but they seemed to be swimming in circles and not doing much else.

'Cyril, would you dive down close to the plinth and see if you can spot a keyhole? We really must find it quickly,' said Oberon, ruffling his white feathers.

'Yes, of course,' said Cyril. 'I'll need to dive from the very top of the statue so as to go down as deep as possible. Then I will need to turn very quickly to come up for another dive. Hmmm, it's such a tight space I might actually break my beak, especially if I accidently hit the plinth itself or the pond floor,' said the heron.

'Yes, yes, that would be dreadful, of course. However, we really do need to see what's down there,' urged the owl. 'Don't worry about your beak. Ernie will heal any injuries.'

Cyril frowned. He wasn't happy at the thought of having his beak broken again, but he knew he was the only one who could dive – after all, he was a diving bird. If he could find the right spot, then Ernie and the goldfish could insert and turn the crystal key and open the door. What a piece of luck that they had found the crystal key stuck in the well bucket at the end of the garden.

'I'll get started, then,' said Cyril. 'Goldfish, please stay out of the way, in case I stab you by accident.'

It was just before dawn when the animals and birds gathered to watch Cyril dive. He had to angle his dive wide enough to avoid hitting the outer rim of the fountain. Then he had to curve his dive inwards again to get as close to the base as possible to see what was there. He would probably have to do this several times to find exactly where the keyhole was.

Cyril tucked his wings in tightly and took a deep breath. He leapt up gracefully, turned swiftly over and shot down like a long, feathered dart. He entered the water with hardly a sound or a splash. After a few seconds he popped up and returned to the top of the statue, shaking out his feathers.

'I couldn't see anything that time. I'll try again,' said Cyril, and he prepared for dive number two. After four dives, there was still nothing to report. The fifth time however, he took longer to resurface and the residents were starting to worry about him.

'Ernie, swim down and see what's happened to Cyril. Please hurry, he's taking a long time,' urged the Brigadier.

'Hurry, hurry!' repeated the owl.

Timber and Dougal moved to the edge of the pond, trying to see what was happening underwater. It was too dark to make anything out. The frog bobbed down to look and the goldfish followed. They all popped up together as Cyril reappeared, gasping for air.

'Found it!' he gulped. 'I've found it!'

He landed on the grass to dry off.

'I used my beak to scratch off some moss and mud at the base to get a better look. There is a small keyhole, which should take the crystal key. It is quite low down and the rest of the moss, mud and grime will need to be removed first. It's all rather gritty and grubby. I think this could be it!'

'This is amazing!' said Dougal.

'Thank heavens!' said Oberon.

'Let's get cracking,' said Timber, delighted. 'Cyril will give you directions,' he said to the goldfish.

After a few words with the heron, the four goldfish went down to the base of the plinth. They used their tails to speed-fan the area, causing the mud and grime to slowly come away and fully expose the key hole. Ernie also helped. With his long, sticky tongue, the frog licked off tiny dead insects that had been clogging the entrance. The newly polished keyhole sparkled just like the crystal key. It was time for the next step.

Chapter Five

RECOVERING THE SCROLL

'We must get the crystal key as quickly as possible,' said the Brigadier.

'No problem. I can get it whenever we're ready,' said Sylvie. 'I'll slip into Jemima's room and take it from her bedside table.'

'Right,' said Timber, 'let's get on with our next task: getting the scroll.' He wondered how they would feel if the plinth turned out to be empty. And he wondered, too, how they would take it out without tearing it. He eyed Teddy and Eldric, who had been thinking the same thing.

'I think Ernie and the goldfish will have to do the important bit this time,' said Teddy.

Everyone looked uneasy. How would a frog and four goldfish get the scroll?

'First of all we have to figure out how they will *turn* the key, then open the door and take the scroll out safely, then bring it to the surface before it dissolves, oh, and not be seen by any of Worfeus' spies. Hmmm, tricky.'

'Don't worry, everyone, we have a plan,' said Ernie in a loud voice. Eldric raised one of his eyebrows and peered at him.

'You have? Great! Let's hear it then.'

'We will wait at the base of the plinth when one of you drops the key very carefully into the water so it falls down right in front of the keyhole,' explained Ernie. 'We'll move quickly to push the key into the hole. Then the goldfish will swim at super-speed around the key, forcing it to turn in the lock. Ta-daaa! Easy!'

'Yes, if Cyril *dives* down *with* the key, he might actually stab one of you accidentally or shoot straight past the keyhole and get stuck in the mud, so it can't be done that way,' said Eldric, thinking out loud.

'And he couldn't stay under water as long as you or the goldfish can,' said Norville, nodding at Ernie.

'Very good,' said Timber. 'Are you sure you can work together like that?'

'We'll do our very best,' said Ernie enthusiastically.

'Yes, it is a good idea, Ernie,' said Oberon. 'But if

you drop the key, will you be able to pick it up again and put it in the keyhole by yourself?'

All eyes turned once again towards the frog.

'Em, maybe just the once,' said Ernie.

'What do you mean, just the once?' asked Norville, rubbing his nose.

'I should be able to pick it up with my tongue, but as it is crystal, it will be heavy. I don't think I'll be able to lift it a second time …' Ernie's voice petered out. He was really hoping he wouldn't fail. This was so important to everyone.

'OK, then, we need to get this right the first time, and if not, then absolutely on the second try,' said the Brigadier firmly.

They decided to borrow the key as soon as the Grindles went out shopping. It was important that the children and the adults didn't know what they were up to – not just yet, anyway. If they did, they might decide to take the key and the scroll and perhaps put them somewhere out of the residents' reach.

The cats ran inside to fetch the key. The garden birds spread out among the trees around the garden to watch for spying magpies or crows. Luckily there were none about. Sylvie picked up the key and ran back outside.

Cyril took the key in his beak and perched directly above where the keyhole was. When Ernie and the goldfish were ready, he dropped the key straight down. It twinkled as it made a little splash on entering the water. It still sparkled as it went down, down, sinking slowly into the darker, deeper water, towards the waiting frog and goldfish. Just as it reached them, they moved quickly to nudge it into place, into the keyhole. But the goldfish were over-excited and they swam too quickly. Their movements sent the key spiralling out of reach. Ernie popped up to tell the others.

'I'll see if I can pick it up. Sorry, everyone, it really was more difficult than we thought,' said Ernie.

'Don't worry, Ernie. We know you can do it,' said Timber, trying to keep his spirits up. Everyone held their breath as Ernie swam down and tried to lift the key with his tongue. He was so very nearly successful, but it was really heavy and the pain in his mouth was terrible. The goldfish tried to help him, but in their eagerness they knocked it right out of his mouth. Down it sank to the bottom of the pond. Ernie came to the surface looking very upset. The goldfish popped up beside him.

'I'm so very sorry,' said Ernie.

'It wasn't Ernie's fault. We knocked it out of his mouth by accident. It was too heavy for any of us to carry. We're so sorry,' said Gilda. The fish dipped down below the surface again.

'Oh, dear,' whispered Cindy.

'Uh oh,' muttered Norville.

Eldric rolled his eyes.

'Never mind, never mind,' said Ramona, bouncing forward. 'Tell the goldfish to nudge it off the floor and onto your back, Ernie. Then you can push off the floor with your feet, just like all rabbits do.' She gave a little demonstration of this. 'Then swim straight for the keyhole,' said Ramona, making it sound easy. They knew they had to get it right.

'That sounds like it might work,' said Timber.

'Well, well, a bunny with brains,' said Eldric, his mood improving quickly.

'Watch it, foxy, my big feet would just love some new target practice!' replied Ramona with a naughty grin. The residents were glad of a little joke. Then it was back to the task. Ernie bobbed down to the bottom of the pond again. Everyone leaned forward at the edge of the pond, hoping to see something soon.

Ernie did as Ramona had suggested. He burrowed into the sandy floor under the key and the goldfish fanned the water until it was nudged into place on his back. Then Ernie kicked off with the key and swam steadily towards the lock. But very soon the key felt heavy, too heavy. He swam bravely, kicking as hard as he could. The goldfish tried to fan the water beneath him, hoping it would help. Ernie thought he could just make it.

He was right in front of the lock when he realised the key was lying on its side. How would they turn it the right way around so it would fit? He struggled to stay in position beside the keyhole, wondering what to do. Out of the blue, approaching from above, a large white dart appeared, heading straight for Ernie. The frog saw the torpedo approaching and he froze, floating beside the lock.

Having landed on the pond, Serena Swan put her head under water and saw the frog's dilemma. Timber asked Cyril to dive one more time to help them out. He zoomed into the water hoping to snatch the key off Ernie's back and with a bit of luck, shove it into the keyhole before he ran out of air, or stabbed poor Ernie at the same time! It was a big risk. Luckily, it worked,

and at last, the key was in the keyhole.

'We've done it!' he cried, gasping for breath, when he came to the surface.

'Great! Now Ernie and the goldfish only have to *turn* the key,' said Timber.

Their smiles vanished as everyone wondered if the little pond dwellers would be able to manage the next step. While Ernie kept the key in place with his feet, the goldfish took up their positions. With a wink and a bubble and a flick of their tails, they all started swimming in a clockwise motion around the key, rapidly building up to super-speed.

They whizzed around the key, faster and faster, circling again and again. Soon, little waves appeared on the surface of the pond. The residents knew then that the fish must be close. Round and round they continued, many, many times. They were getting very dizzy, when finally the crystal key began to turn, CLICK, CLICK, CLICKETY-CLINK, CLICKETY-CLINK, CLUNK!

The little square door in the bottom of the plinth popped open. Ernie swam closer to take a look inside. A light shone out of the little enchanted safe. It was a warm, soft light that surrounded the scroll. It dimmed slowly until it went out. And there it was – Wanda's secret scroll. It was wrapped in what seemed to be curly leaves that protected its precious contents. It appeared to be in perfect condition. Nothing was ripped, torn or blemished. It wasn't even watermarked. It was said to contain a powerful spell, so no doubt the leaves had been enchanted too. The goldfish looked on from a little distance, too nervous to go any closer. Ernie was excited and curious, but he didn't like to touch it either – not yet. He had to tell the others first.

'It's there, it's there, the scroll!' he cried. His bulging eyes nearly popped with excitement. The residents wanted to jump and cheer, but they didn't want to attract attention.

'When Ernie gets the scroll to the surface, I think we should take it to the fairy house,' said Timber. 'After we examine it, we can decide where to hide it.'

'Yes, I must look at it immediately, and the key too,' said Oberon.

'Who can scoop up the scroll without damaging it?' asked Teddy. 'It might fall apart.'

'Well, I can get the key,' said Cyril.

'And I can pick up the scroll once Ernie brings it to the surface,' said Dougal.

'Yes, of course,' said the Brigadier. 'Spaniels are very good at carrying birds and, eh, lots of things, without tearing or breaking them, ahem, yes.'

'Really?' asked Waldorf, shaking his tail feathers. Being a wood pigeon, he didn't like the thought of being inside a dog's mouth.

'Really,' confirmed Eldric, who had seen this many times.

'Good idea, Dougal,' said Timber. 'Now, bring us the scroll, Ernie.'

Ernie smiled his happiest smile ever and bobbed back down to retrieve the scroll. After a few fantails and more bubble blowing, the goldfish and the frog eased the scroll gently out of the safe. It floated gracefully up to the surface. Dougal jumped into the water and picked it up carefully in his mouth. He swam out of the pond and dashed over to the fairy house, with the cats and dogs all around him. Cyril dived one more time to grab the key.

All the residents crowded into the fairy house. The foxes and owls leaned over the scroll, hoping to decipher it quickly. But it wasn't going to be that simple. Peeling back the curling leaves that surrounded the parchment was weird enough. Oberon gently and carefully removed them, trusting and hoping that the leaves were there only to protect the scroll from damage, and nothing more. He was right. There were no nasty surprises.

The scroll was made up of several pages of strange yet beautiful writing. It was really more like a work of art. The parchment was carefully designed and decorated with many colours and diagrams. Everyone took a quick look, but no one had a clue what any of it could mean.

'This is wonderful,' said the Brigadier, peering at the scroll. 'Well done, everyone!'

'At last, the scroll,' purred Sylvie.

'It's fantastic,' said Timber. He looked at Oberon and Eldric still glued to the scroll, frowning and mumbling. 'Can you understand any of it?'

'Let me look at the key again,' said Oberon, fussing. 'Perhaps I can match some of the inscriptions or symbols. Some of them look similar.'

'Oh, this is really tricky,' groaned Eldric.

After a while, the residents left Timber, Oberon and Eldric to examine the scroll, while they talked about where it should be kept once they had deciphered the spell.

'How about the new duck house on the grassy mound?' asked Norville. 'The ducks aren't back yet, and probably won't be for a while.'

'No, it's too difficult for us to get to it if there's trouble,' said Sylvie, not liking the idea of crossing the water. 'How about somewhere in the house, like in Jemima's old dolls' house, or in Jamie's bean bag? I could rip a little hole in the side of the bean bag and we could stuff the scroll inside?'

'It might get damaged,' said Teddy, 'and the beans will end up all over the floor. Then the Grindles would find it.'

Heads were scratched, paws shuffled, and all the little birds were jabbering in the trees beside the fairy house. There were lots more ideas, but they couldn't find the right solution.

'How about in Ramona's hutch?'

'I don't think so,' said the rabbit sternly.

'Oops, sorry!'

'How about in the chicken coop?'

'How about in one of the birds' nests?' suggested Norville.

'Don't you think the thieving magpies will see it there?' said Waldorf.

'Oh, let's put it back in the pond then!'

They all laughed. Just then, Balthazar, the biggest bee in Grindlewood, flew into the fairy house through the little side window.

'Hello, everyone!' he said cheerfully. 'The hive has just woken up and this is my first spring buzz-around. 'What a lovely bright day it is. Oh, I am really looking forward to this year's Operation Pollination!'

The big friendly bee flew around the fairy house, exercising his sleepy wings.

'I hope you all had a wonderful winter. How is everyone?' He landed back on the windowsill. Everyone stopped what they were doing and looked at Balthazar.

'Well, come on, then, any news?' he asked, smiling at them all.

There, right in front of them, was the answer to their question.

Chapter Six

INTO THE HIVE

The residents were delighted to see Balthazar and they took turns to fill him in on all the events of the past few months.

'Unbelievable!' he said over and over again. 'And everyone is all right?'

'Yes, Balthazar, we are all fine, thanks to Timber's extraordinary bravery and Ernie's special healing powers,' said the Brigadier.

'We also had the Brigadier's clever defence plans,' added Timber.

'And some extraordinary scouting by all the birds,' said Eldric.

'Ahem, ahem,' coughed Norville.

'Oh, and Norville's wonderful hunch,' added Eldric.

'And some very clever thinking by Eldric,' added Norville, smiling at his friend.

'It was a team effort, Balthazar, really it was,' said Timber. 'But the important thing is that we've finally made progress on our quest: we have found Wanda's secret scroll. As you know it contains the only spell that can rid the world of the evil warlock Worfeus. He is still stuck in the forest behind Grindlewood, and we know he is working on his escape. We think he plans to come here and destroy Grindlewood, so we must decipher the spell as quickly as possible in order to stop him, once and for all.'

'Unfortunately, we still have some difficult decoding to do,' said Oberon loudly, interrupting all the chatter. 'The scroll is written in more than one ancient witch language, and I believe the only person who can decipher it is Gildevard, the golden eagle.'

'Do you think you can make that long journey to the cliff top again?' Timber asked the owl.

'Oh, yes, I think I have to. But I cannot take the scroll with me. It could be too easily spotted,' replied the wise owl. 'I will have to persuade Gildevard to come to Grindlewood. That, my friends, could be difficult. But I think this scroll just might be interesting enough to tempt him.'

The owl muttered to himself for a few minutes and

then turned to everyone. 'I will leave tonight. There must be no more delays,' he said. 'While I am away, it is terribly important that no one knows that we have the scroll. Everything depends on it. Take good care of it, Timber, and that crystal key too.'

'Don't worry, Oberon, we have a very clever hiding place in mind for the scroll. The key will be safer back in the house, for the time being,' replied the malamute.

Oberon went to hunt before heading off once again to Gildevard's cliff-top nest. Sylvie returned the key to Jemima's bedroom. Thoughts then turned to protecting the scroll.

'It's just as well we had started to think about where to hide it,' said Cindy.

'I thought Oberon was the expert in all this, this spell stuff,' moaned Norville. 'Now he's heading off again, and who knows how long he will be.'

'Oberon needs some expert help to translate the spell,' said Eldric.

'I hope this visit to the cliff top won't take too long,' said the Brigadier. 'Gildevard may not want to come all the way to Grindlewood, or he might not be at home, which could mean another delay.'

'Don't worry. Oberon will do his best,' said Timber.

'So where will we put the scroll?' asked Dougal.

'Balthazar, would it be possible to hide the scroll in the hive?' asked Timber, turning to the big bee.

'Oh, brilliant!' said Eldric.

'Um, won't it get all sticky with that honey stuff?' asked Dougal.

'It should be protected by those special leaves, Dougal. I'm sure they were carefully chosen and enchanted by Wanda. What do you think, Balthazar?' asked Timber.

'They're very strange leaves. I've never seen anything like them before, but they are so thick and oily, they look like they would protect against just about anything,' said the bee, buzzing around the leaves, prodding them with his little nose.

'I'm glad they've stopped moving,' said Dougal. 'The way they kept rolling around the scroll was really weird.'

'It was Wanda's magic, of course,' said Teddy.

'Now, we have to figure out how to get it into the hive,' said Timber. 'Once inside, the bees will be on guard all the time and we'll be on guard on the outside. I hope this won't disrupt the honey-making, Balthazar?'

'Oh no, we'll be fine,' replied the big bee cheerfully. 'There are so many of us this year we've already started building an extension. We'll just have to make it even bigger now, that's all!'

'Superb!' said the Brigadier. 'Balthazar, if the queen bee agrees, we should get the scroll inside right away.'

Balthazar flew back to the hive and some of the residents left the fairy house. The cats and dogs remained behind to guard the scroll. Dougal found a neat little hiding place under the floorboards and nudged the scroll gently inside. It couldn't be left there for very long, though. Greg had been doing some work on the little house and might easily come across it. If he did, the residents would have no idea when they might get it back. That would be disastrous.

Since the wolf attack in the forest, the garden had been unusually quiet. The few remaining magpies had not been seen at all, nor the giant rat that had escaped a while back. No one was sure just how many crows were still alive because they hadn't been spotted either and it troubled the residents that they didn't know exactly what Worfeus was up to. They certainly didn't want their plans messed up, not by spying magpies.

In fact, Worfeus had sent his magpies on a different mission. He had sent them to find an old acquaintance of his, a buzzard who had a dreadful reputation for lying, cheating and thieving. The two despicable characters had often traded favours in the past, when it suited them, even though they never really trusted each other.

❧

The bees worked tirelessly to finish the hive quickly and after all their work it was the strangest, and probably the largest, beehive ever built. Balthazar was feeling very important as he directed all the bees' activities.

When at last it was ready, the bees were organised into groups to move the scroll, protect the hive, or guard its precious treasure on all fronts. Back in the fairy house, there had been long conversations about how the bees would lift it safely into the hive. As always, the residents came up with a plan. Because Cindy was the smallest cat, she was chosen to take the scroll carefully in her mouth and carry it the short distance to the hedge where the hive was located. Being small, Timber could stand over her to keep the little cat and the scroll out of sight as they moved towards the hive. By now, they knew that the protective leaves would keep it safe in her mouth.

The other cats and dogs would stay close to them as they made the short journey to the hive. The foxes, hedgehog and some of the bigger rabbits would all run and bounce around the garden on lookout duty. The birds would be perched high and low in the trees, watching for trouble. Even the rooster would patrol the yard, as he wanted to play his part like everyone else. The residents were ready.

Ernie was not required for this particular task. Instead, he sat on the highest stone in the rockery trying to catch a little weak spring sunshine. He noticed the butterflies had emerged from their winter sleep in Norville's nest.

Ernie watched them and wondered when the next vision would come – and what it would be. Their visions had helped them in the past and everyone was looking forward to their return, but they were also a bit nervous. Their last few visions had been worrying.

Cindy was especially proud to be chosen to carry the scroll. She had never done anything so important in her life. When they reached the hedge, she jumped onto Timber's back and from there she sprang up to the hive, where it was tucked into the thickest part of the hedge. She balanced gingerly on some thin branches. As she wobbled there, holding the scroll carefully in her mouth, the bees swarmed out. There were so many bees Cindy disappeared for a moment in a buzzing blur of black and yellow. Then hundreds of bees flew under the scroll and lifted it up and carried it into the hive. Balthazar and some of the bigger bees gave a final shove from behind to make sure it was fully concealed. At last it was safe.

The animals left the hive and went about their normal routines. The bees would look after the scroll. Nothing else could be done until Oberon returned with Gildevard. They all wondered if the eagle really would come. And what would they do if he refused?

Chapter Seven

GILDEVARD, THE GOLDEN EAGLE

The butterflies' first message of spring was bewildering:

The glorious one must come to the well
We three must sing to cast the spell!

Eldric thought that 'the glorious one' must be the eagle.

'That's the first mention of the spell,' said Timber.

'Yes, it means we're on the right track, I think,' said the Brigadier.

'What's that about singing?' asked Dougal.

'Oh, dear,' said Norville, 'it's another puzzle.'

'Yes, it is, but at least we know what the first part means,' said Eldric. They trundled off together, discussing what the second part of the message could mean. Could the butterflies really sing? No one knew the answer.

It was taking Oberon a lot longer to reach Gildevard's nest this time around. Bad weather meant he had to stop and take shelter more often than he would have liked. Finally he reached his destination, but this time Gildevard was not at home. Oberon had no choice but to wait.

The eagle's nest was large and scruffy, sitting high up on a cliff. Despite the bitter cold, and a brisk whistling wind, Oberon didn't dare climb in without permission. He snuggled down close to the nest to try to keep warm and get some sleep. He woke up with a start to find a kestrel pecking at his tail feathers.

'Stop that at once,' shouted Oberon. 'How dare you peck me like that! I am a friend of Gildevard's. Who are you, and what do you want?'

'I am Gildevard's apprentice and I am keeping watch over his nest while he is away. What do *you* want with him?' asked the tough-talking kestrel.

'My business is private and urgent. When will he be back?' tooted Oberon.

'I don't know. He goes on retreats, to think and to study. He doesn't even know himself when he will return. He could be gone quite a while,' replied the kestrel. 'But I might be able to get a message to him, if you just tell me what it is about.'

'I will find him myself, if you just tell me where he is,' replied Oberon crossly.

'That's not allowed. Gildevard does not want to be disturbed, except for real emergencies.'

'This *is* a real emergency,' said Oberon, finding it hard not to lose his temper. 'Please tell him that Oberon Owl needs to speak with him urgently on the same matter we discussed recently. He will understand.'

'Oh, very well then,' said the kestrel.

He flew up and disappeared into the cloudy sky and biting mountain winds.

The owl waited for another whole day. He was getting more and more anxious with every passing hour. Finally he saw them, the eagle and the kestrel, soaring high in the sky, circling slowly, down and down until they reached the nest.

'Gildevard, thank you for coming back to see me. I'm sorry I had to disturb your studies,' said Oberon.

'Kelvin said the matter was urgent,' said Gildevard, sounding a little less stuffy than usual. Oberon glanced at the kestrel before saying anything more. Gildevard understood that look and dismissed the kestrel with a nod. Kelvin was a little annoyed that he was to be left out of their conversation, but he flew off as directed.

'Gildevard, do you remember that key I showed you, the crystal key from Grindlewood garden?'

'Of course I do. It was very interesting. In fact, I have been revising that ancient language since you were last here,' replied the golden eagle. 'Is there more?'

'Yes, we have now found the scroll – *Wanda's secret scroll*,' whispered Oberon. Gildevard raised a thickly feathered eyebrow and leaned forward, looking deep into Oberon's eyes.

'Go on,' said the eagle.

'I believe it contains a most important spell,' said Oberon, 'the only spell that can destroy the evil Worfagon leader, Worfeus.' Oberon barely whispered the warlock's name, as if in fear of it. 'Some of the spell is written in the same ancient tongue as the inscription on the crystal key, and some of it in another language, which I don't recognise. That's why we need your help,' explained Oberon. 'There are also some strange symbols and diagrams scattered throughout the pages of parchment, and we don't know what they mean either. It is quite a puzzle.'

'Pages of parchment, you say. Hmm, I see you don't have the scroll with you,' said Gildevard.

'I'm sure you understand,' replied Oberon. 'I didn't want to risk losing it or attracting the attention of Worfeus' spying magpies and crows. There is no way they would miss it if it were sticking out of my beak or talons.'

Gildevard nodded.

'Actually, I was hoping to invite you back to Grindlewood so you could examine it in safety,' said Oberon.

The snowy owl shifted uneasily on his feet as Gildevard hunched down in his nest and closed his eyes. The owl had to wait patiently, knowing that the golden eagle didn't like to be rushed.

'Oberon, that ancient language was only ever used by a very old magical clan – the Wandeleis. They were a people very loyal to the Forest Queen, and rumour has it that there aren't too many of them left. I'm sure you came across the Forest Queen in your history studies.' The owl nodded. The Forest Queen was often mentioned.

'As you probably know, the Wandeleis lived in

and around Grindlewood and it became known as an important magical place. But their peace-loving ways were a disadvantage when it came to protecting their traditions, their treasures, and even their queen from the warring Worfagons. The Wandeleis waited too long to fight back. As a result, the Worfagons ransacked the queen's dwelling, stole many valuable and magical possessions and then cursed the queen to grow like a tree in the ground for centuries. I should think Worfeus will want to finish this business once and for all. That's why this scroll will be so important to him, and also why it is so important for all of Grindlewood.'

Oberon listened politely.

'After I saw the crystal key, I suspected something more might turn up. Yes, I will return with you to Grindlewood. We shall eat, sleep and depart at dawn. Come, Oberon, join me for supper.' The golden eagle summoned the kestrel to bring them some food.

'One more question, Oberon,' said the golden eagle, making room for the owl. 'Do you have butterflies in the garden, a trio perhaps?'

'Yes, we do. Why do you ask?'

'And how long have they been there?'

'About five or six years. It's hard to believe,' replied Oberon.

'Yes, a long time for butterflies to live,' said Gildevard. 'The Wandelei people admired butterflies for their beauty and grace, and also for their simplicity. They often enchanted them, believing they could not be corrupted by anyone.'

Oberon opened his eyes wide. 'But of course!' he cried.

'Hmm, this will be very interesting, very interesting indeed,' said Gildevard, looking very pleased.

Oberon was also very pleased.

While the residents waited anxiously for Oberon and Gildevard, the garden was beginning to burst with spring activity. The spring weather was very changeable, but the evenings were getting longer and the days were a little warmer. Many of the birds were busy preparing new nests to welcome their offspring and the bees who weren't on duty guarding the scroll were venturing out of the hive in search of pollen. The ducks arrived with the swans for a swim on the pond, but they weren't quite ready to return, even though they were thrilled with the new duck house.

The Easter holidays were at the end of March, just

a couple of weeks after Jamie's tenth birthday. The week before the birthday party, Greg was very busy in his workshop, hammering and chiselling away, making lots of furniture and also making Jamie's birthday present. He was building his son a rowing boat. The family were planning to take sailing lessons on Lindon Lake over the summer, and any practice on their own pond would be really worthwhile.

Lots of the children's friends came for Jamie's birthday party, and because it was so close to Easter, Gloria organised a chocolate-egg hunt. This was great fun and even some of the pets joined in, causing complete chaos!

Ramona was delighted to see her friend Abigail Allnutt again. She bounced around the garden, letting all the children chase her. Whenever the boys kicked Jamie's football into the bushes, Ramona kicked the ball back with her strong hind legs. The children howled with laughter. All the birds were singing happily in the trees and the blackbirds gave a stunning performance. Over in the pond, the goldfish showed off with some speed-swimming and tail-stands. Ernie performed some amazing acrobatics, hopping around the lily pads and stones.

In the yard the chickens were joined by the rooster for an afternoon dance, and they flapped, fluttered, squawked and shook their tails to great effect. The children's parents couldn't quite understand all the commotion, but the children thought it was hilarious. The sunshine didn't last long, though, and soon the storm clouds gathered. The children ran inside for a lovely party tea as the sky darkened, the wind whipped up and the rain came pouring down.

It had been a fun-filled spring day, in total contrast to what was about to unfold.

Chapter Eight

TROUBLE'S BREWING

In the days after Jamie's birthday party, the garden seemed too quiet. There was no sign of Worfeus' armies of cantankerous birds and grotesque rats, and although this was good news, the residents were becoming edgy.

'I think it's time I went back there to see what's going on. There's no point in just sitting here, waiting for Oberon. Everyone will go crazy soon,' said Pippa.

The residents looked down at their tiny ladybird friend. They didn't like to say it, but it did seem like a good idea.

'That's very brave of you, Pippa, but please don't feel you have to go. It's very dangerous,' said the Brigadier.

'I know, Brigadier, but it has to be me. Everyone else would be easily spotted. Anyway, I have some friends who could come with me this time, some new ladybirds who hatched in Norville's nest.'

'Oh? Tell us about your friends, Pippa,' said Timber.

'Well, I thought if there were a few of us flying around together, we would have a better chance of seeing something. Anyway, it can feel rather spooky in there, all on your own.'

'Can we trust them, Pippa?' asked Timber. 'It's important no one else knows that we have the scroll or what we are planning.'

'Oh yes, we can trust them,' said Pippa readily.

'What makes you think so?' asked Teddy.

'Em, em …' Pippa couldn't really explain why she trusted them, she just did. Her plan was starting to sound a bit fuzzy.

But Pippa kept insisting, so, after further discussion, it was agreed the ladybirds could go, but there would be no mention of scrolls or spells, magic or warlocks to Pippa's friends. Only Pippa would know the real reason for going into the forest. Bryony Barn Owl would carry the ladybirds to the edge of the forest. They would need to save their energy for snooping around. They decided to return to the forest that night.

The four blackbirds and two wood pigeons headed off first and perched in different trees along the route.

They wanted to be sure it was clear of Worfeus' spies. The trees were strangely empty. The Brigadier and Timber carefully explained to Pippa and her ladybird friends what they were to do. Bryony carried them safely out of the garden, over the field and up to the edge of the forest.

'Off you go, now,' Bryony whispered. 'I'll be waiting close by.'

The tiny ladybirds flew around for a while, following any scents or sounds they picked up. Eventually they reached the warlock's lair.

As luck would have it, they were just in time to see quite a lot. Worfeus was marching around the cauldron, frowning and scratching his long pointy chin.

'That's it!' he cried out. 'I have it figured out now! Just a few more nasty ingredients and one long chant of a particularly crafty spell and I'll have what I need,' said Worfeus, as he sneered at the hags. The warlock suddenly picked up a battered crow and two injured magpies and flung them into the cauldron. The pot hissed and spat. He whirled around the frightened old witches, excited by his plans. He bent down to catch the last buck-toothed rat snoozing near the fire and tossed it into the sizzling cauldron as well. The hags eyed each other anxiously and stirred even harder.

'That's it, old witches – stir, stir, stir. We're cooking up something special tonight!' he bellowed, standing behind them, watching the smoke and bubbles rise from the pot.

The ladybirds watched it all too, terrified. But that wasn't the end of it. After a few more minutes of very hard stirring, Worfeus lunged at the two hags and flung them kicking and screaming into the cauldron. The foul brew exploded into massive bubbles as the witches were swallowed up. It continued to pop, crackle and hiss for a few minutes before settling down to a steady simmer.

Worfeus began to chant a spell, and as he did so, the big black pot threw up more smelly smoke and peculiar brown bubbles burst on the scummy surface. Now and again a screech or a squeal broke through and was then drowned in the boiling broth. The smell was atrocious, like stink bombs and dung all mixed up together. Something dreadful was being created in the cauldron, something truly monstrous.

'Valerius!' roared Worfeus, stomping around the cauldron again. 'Come here at once!'

The vole appeared out of the bushes. The ladybirds hadn't heard a peep, yet he had been so, so close.

'Yes, master,' squeaked the grovelling vole. 'What is your wish, master?'

'Stir the cauldron, stir it well, my ugly goblin-vole. For this new spell of mine will create the most foul and ferocious creatures to do my work. The scroll simply must be in that garden and my ferocious five shall go and FIND IT!' he roared and shook his fists at the sky.

Valerius replied with his usual nod, but he was annoyed at having to stir the big pot now that the last two hags were gone. He grimaced and snarled, sweating and groaning as he stirred and stirred and stirred. He knew this could go on for many hours, until the proper brew had been reached and many spells had been chanted. Eventually the five would be ready, though – big, ugly and ferocious – and under Worfeus' command.

'My fiendish ferrets will do the job that all the other idiots could not! They will not fail, they will NOT BE

STOPPED! Not until I get what I want from that garden! I want that scroll. I want the spells I know are in that scroll. I want the queen's jewels. I want all the ancient magic that is hidden in that garden, I want it all! And then I shall destroy Grindlewood for ever and all those do-gooders too!'

Worfeus paced up and down, shaking his head and ranting all the while. He had thought it would be easy to get his hands on the scroll once he had disposed of that silly little witch, five years ago. But because she had left so much trouble behind her, those clever enchantments to help her garden friends, the task of finding the scroll had become surprisingly difficult for him.

Without warning, Worfeus started wincing and jerking about. He roared in protest, 'No, no, not now. This is not meant to happen any more, I fixed that problem! Noooo! Aaaaahh!'

As the shape-shifting continued, the warlock tried desperately to steady himself.

'By the time these fer-ferrets are ready for action, I just might have my own escape po-potion ready. And then I can leave this for-forest AT LAST!' he roared. Then he howled and growled, tottering on feet that looked very strange. They were turning into wolf paws. 'F-faster Val-Valerius, f-f-faster,' he ordered the weary vole.

'Master, I need to take a break,' moaned Valerius.

'N-nonsense, you will not st-stop until I say s-so, and I D-D-DON'T S-S-SAY SOOOO!'

'Master, I see you are about to turn back into a wolf. May I just say before you completely transform …'

'WH-WH-WHAT, WHAT, you annoying little gog-glob-blob-gob-bloblin?' thundered Worfeus. As his face turned into a long wolf muzzle, his speech became very confused. Changing into a wolf was very painful and troublesome.

'I thought you should know, master, that there are several ladybirds back there in the bushes,' said Valerius.

'WHAAAT? LADYBIRDS? HERE? They must be s-s-spies! Are those garden do-gooders actually spying on ME?'

'Shall I deal with them myself, or would you like to, master?' asked Valerius calmly, knowing what the response would be.

'G-G-GOOOO! Find the spies!' Worfeus bellowed back and the vole got a rest from stirring the cauldron after all. He scurried back over to the bushes where he had spotted the ladybirds.

Valerius was on them in a flash. Knowing he couldn't catch them all, the crafty vole pounced on the ones that moved first, as they scattered to hide. Some of them were caught and Valerius munched on them greedily. Others flew sideways and also got caught. Others, including Pippa, flew upwards and out of the vole's reach. They continued flying higher and higher, until they could fly no further. It was their only chance of escape.

Bryony was alert. With her keen owl eyes she soon saw there was trouble. She zoomed in from the edge of the forest, whipping around in circles so the remaining ladybirds could land safely on her back, and then she carried them out of the forest and back to safety.

Valerius trotted back to his master. The warlock, now a scraggy, grumpy wolf, was waiting beside the cauldron. The vole stood in front him and spat a couple of times.

'What are you doing now?' roared Worfeus.

'I had a little snack of ladybirds. But I thought you might like to have one too. So here she is, still alive, I think.' He hoped to impress his master by delivering the ladybird alive for questioning. A bout of torturing usually pleased the evil warlock.

'Well, well, well, you're in a bit of bother, aren't you? I think you will tell me everything I want to know.' Worfeus snarled, poking the little insect with his paws. 'But first,' he said, turning to Valerius again, 'find me that barn owl, the one that was hiding in the trees at the edge of the forest.' The vole looked surprised. 'Yes, that's right. You idiot! You didn't even see her, did you? She's much more likely to cause us trouble than these silly little insects. Go on, find out what she was up to!'

Valerius raced out of sight, even though he knew the barn owl would be long gone. The warlock turned his attention back to the defenceless ladybird.

The residents packed in to the fairy house as Bryony flew in through the open window. She landed softly in their midst. The remaining ladybirds flew out of her feathers and on to the floor. Everyone noticed straight away that some were missing.

'What happened, Bryony?' asked Timber.

'They were discovered and some of them were

caught,' explained the barn owl.

'It was the vole, that horrible vole,' cried Pippa. 'He spotted us and pounced on my friends. Only half of us got away. Oh, it was terrible and it's all my fault.'

The residents were horrified. Before anyone could say anything, Pippa rushed to tell them the rest.

'Worfeus is cooking something terrible in his cauldron. He said that his ferocious five would be ready in a few days and that they would do the job the others failed to do.' She took a deep breath. There was more to tell. 'He is working on a potion that will free him from the forest, and he hopes it will be ready in time so he can follow the five beasts to the garden and get the scroll himself.'

Hearing this, some of the ducks fainted, and Ernie's creamy tummy turned a bright shade of green, just like the rest of him.

'What are these beasts?' asked Dougal.

Pippa was trying to remember. 'Something that sounds like forests, no, furries, no, no, ferrets. Yes, that's it – five ferocious ferrets.'

'Oh no,' moaned Eldric. 'I hate ferrets. They're very nasty.'

'Nothing we can't handle, eh, Timber?' said the Brigadier, trying to sound cheery. This was not the time to start panicking.

'Of course we can. We can handle anything that warlock sends our way,' said the big dog confidently. 'Now that we know what's happening, we need a good plan.'

'Right,' said the Brigadier, 'another plan, yes.'

'I think this scroll means more to Worfeus than we already know about,' said Timber. 'He's obsessed with it.'

'I agree,' said Eldric.

'If he is such a powerful and evil warlock, why does he need it, except to stop us using it?' asked Teddy.

'Exactly what I was wondering,' said Timber.

There was no more for them to do tonight. Bryony whisked the little insects off to rest and the other residents began plotting the next defence of the garden. It would need to be a very good defence indeed.

Jemima and Abigail often did their homework together after school and then retreated to Jemima's bedroom to read up on magic and spells.

'More books, Jemima!' said her mother, as the two

girls climbed the stairs, each carrying a heavy pile of old books.

'My granddad gave me all these books, Mrs Grindle. They were in the cellar of his antique shop,' said Abigail cheerfully.

'Mr Allnutt's cellar is amazing, Mum, and all these old books are great. They're full of great stories about magic, and, eh, lots of stuff.' Jemima thought it best not to mention witches and warlocks. She didn't want to worry her mother. The two girls hurried upstairs. They had a lot of reading to do.

Jamie was going to try some 'talking lessons' with Timber. He was only going to teach his malamute from now on, as trying to teach all three dogs at the same time had been much too confusing for everyone. He hoped the lessons would be easier that way.

Despite what seemed like enormous tasks – reading lots of big old books and trying to teach a dog to talk – the children felt sure that one of them would figure out something important soon. It had been much easier to understand and accept the good magic they had seen performed by the frog, the butterflies and the goldfish. They had more difficult questions now, though, questions about the forest, the dark magic of the roots and vines, the wolf, and the ranting warlock. And what were all the animals up to? Could the children really do anything to help? Events of recent days were some of the strangest Jamie and Jemima had ever known.

Chapter Nine

THE FEROCIOUS FIVE

The wet and windy weather never seemed to stop and this weekend was no exception. The dark days continued despite the fact that it was well and truly springtime. The Grindles wrapped up well against the weather. They were going to the local farmers' market, which had become a favourite weekend trip. Afterwards, they would take the dogs for their usual Saturday walk.

Deep in the forest, the cauldron wasn't bubbling any more. It was sending pillars of dark purple smoke high into the air, wisping through the tops of the leafless trees, straight up to the clouds, turning them a strange hue of lilac-grey. The dark clouds blocked out most of the daylight and made everything look gloomy.

The animals had noticed a peculiar odour wafting

its way from the forest. The stink had been in the air for a couple of days. There was no doubt that the ferrets were nearly ready.

There was a distinct air of unease around the garden once the dogs had gone for their walk. The residents could sense the trouble.

They heard them first, screeching wildly as they bounded through the neighbouring field. The birds and insects flew quickly to the higher branches of the trees. The animals ran to their dwellings and even the cats ran into the house and watched from there. They would not be able to defend the garden without the dogs, not this time.

The five ferocious ferrets charged through the hedges and borders around the garden. Snarling, snivelling, and wild-eyed, they were formidable beasts. They were much bigger than normal ferrets, at least three times the size, with bulging muscles and long, hooked teeth. They bolted around the garden, their nostrils spread wide as they sniffed and searched for something. Their wild eyes darted quickly about as they checked every corner of the garden.

The ferrets scratched at the ground, rummaged in the bushes, tore through the flowerbeds, and then they

all stopped. They looked at the pond and together they raced over. They jumped into the water and swam quickly around and around, ducking and diving, sending the goldfish dashing for cover.

Ernie was already well hidden in his rock cave. Safe and sound, he watched the ferrets zooming through the water, scratching and clawing at the base of the fountain. Their digging was so frantic that they managed to knock it over. The stone fountain, and the statue on top, fell slowly to one side until only the head, shoulders and tarnished little trumpet were left sticking out of the water. The rest of the sculpture was lodged in the mud, wedged between a few rocks on the pond bed.

With the impact of the fall, the little door in the plinth fell open. The ferrets rushed forward to look in, but of course it was empty. They swam quickly to the surface, looked around again and then left the pond altogether. They bounded back through the hedges, over the field, back to the forest, as quickly as they had come.

The residents peeped out from their hideouts and breathed a sigh of relief. Some of the animals gathered to talk.

'Worfeus was very keen on the pond again,' said Eldric.

'I think he knows that the scroll was hidden there,' said Teddy.

'Yes, there were attacks on the pond before, but this time, they seemed very sure about the base of the fountain,' said Sylvie. 'Pippa, did you say anything to your little friends about where the scroll had been hidden?'

'Oh, dear, I might have said something when we arrived in the forest. My friends were surprised by just how awful it was. I tried to warn them of the danger without actually telling them any secrets, but once we got there, I really had to tell them something. It was only fair.' Pippa knew she had made a big mistake. 'But, but I knew the scroll had been moved, and, and I never said where it had been moved to,' she added.

'Oh, for goodness sake,' said all three foxes.

'My, oh, my,' squeaked Norville nervously. 'That wasn't very clever, was it?'

'Stay calm, everyone,' said Balthazar, landing on Teddy's head and sounding a bit like the Brigadier. 'We know the scroll is safe, and so are we. Luckily the ferrets didn't want a fight, and just as well too, while the dogs are out.'

'I'm so sorry,' said Pippa. 'I didn't mean to cause any trouble. I was just trying to help. Oh, I've made such a mess of everything.'

'It's all right, Pippa, you were very brave to go into the forest,' said Balthazar gently, but he was just as worried as everyone else.

'This is not all right!' said Norville crossly. 'Ferrets are very nasty and they're not afraid of a fight. Why, they're not even afraid of my spikes! I know because I've had to defend myself from ferrets before, and those ferrets came out of the warlock's cauldron, remember! They're monstrous!'

'I'm afraid Worfeus must have got the information from one of the ladybirds,' said Teddy. 'We must be ready for the ferrets to return. We'll talk again later when the dogs get back.'

'Let's hope they're back soon,' said Sylvie.

The anxious residents went off about their business.

The dogs barked loudly as they bounded into the garden. Timber lapped up gallons of water straight away, while the Brigadier headed straight for the kennel to snooze. Dougal had a quick slurpy drink and waited for Timber to do their late-afternoon patrol together. The Brigadier didn't go on many patrols any more.

He left those duties to the younger dogs.

Teddy told them all about the ferrets' sniff-hunt, as he called it. Eldric, Norville and Ramona quickly joined them, so they went into the fairy house to talk.

'Wow, all this happened when we were out!' said Dougal. 'The magpies must be watching us again.'

'They were probably waiting for us to go out,' agreed Timber.

'I didn't see any of them,' said Waldorf, landing on the windowsill. 'In fact, another wood pigeon told me he saw a few magpies heading north a few days ago and again early this morning. They were ragged, angry-looking birds, probably some of Worfeus' old magpies.'

'Hmm, I wonder where they were going,' said Timber. 'We'll have to avoid going on long walks for the next few days.'

'How do we do that?' asked Dougal.

'It might be easier than you think,' said the Brigadier, joining the group. 'I just heard the Grindles say they are going away for a few days.'

'Uh oh! They might decide to put you in kennels,' said Teddy.

'Oh no,' said the Brigadier. 'I hadn't thought of that.'

'Kennels?' asked Dougal.

'Very boring, Dougal, very boring,' said the Brigadier.

'That would be a big problem,' said Timber. 'We need to be here in the garden.'

He wondered how to get that message across to the Grindles. Perhaps he could try to 'talk' to the children after all.

Jamie and Jemima came into the garden as the animals scampered off, all except the pets. The children noticed that the statue was on its side and wandered over to take a look. Greg and Gloria followed them. They had noticed it from an upstairs window and Greg had brought his waders with him.

'I'll see if I can straighten this fountain up. Stand back everyone. If it falls, you'll all get splashed.'

'What could have knocked it over?' asked Gloria.

Jamie looked at Jemima. They said nothing.

'Oh, I don't know. Maybe the bottom of the pond is a bit soft or something,' said Greg. He tried to lift it. When that didn't work, he tried pushing it up. 'No, it's much too heavy,' he said. 'I might ask Arthur to help me wedge it out later. It's still intact, though – no broken bits anywhere.' Greg waded slowly back out of the water.

'Greg, look over here,' said Gloria, pointing to the messed-up flowerbeds.

'That's odd,' said Greg. 'Just look at those claw marks. The cats' claws aren't that big, surely.'

'I hope it's not the rats again! I thought we were finished with that problem.'

'They can't be rats, Mum, the claws are way too long,' said Jamie, sounding like an expert. He really did watch a lot of nature programmes on television. 'Maybe it was a badger or a ferret, or something.' He looked at Jemima.

The dogs barked at the mention of ferrets. Greg gave them a thoughtful look. Jamie stared at Timber. The big dog pawed at the ground; that was his 'danger' signal.

'Hmm, I think we'll leave the dogs here after all,' said Greg. 'I'm sure Arthur won't mind feeding them when we're away. It's only a few days. He looked after the Brigadier and Sylvie for five years without any problems.'

'I don't want to leave them here while we're staying with the Finlays,' said Jemima. 'Can't we stay here, even one or two nights?'

'We don't want them getting into fights with ferrets, Dad,' pleaded Jamie.

'Absolutely not! We discussed this already. Both of you will be staying with the Finlays. During the day, you can come over with Arthur to feed them. And, as you'll be on mid-term break, you can help Arthur around the farm too. You'll have a great time.'

The children didn't look at all pleased.

'Don't worry,' said Greg. 'The cats will use the catflap as they always do and the dogs will be fine in the kennel at night and in the garden during the day. It's what they always do.'

'Yes, it'll be fun staying on the farm and it's only for a few days,' added their mum. 'Arthur knows exactly how to take care of all the animals, including the, eh, wildlife. *And*, you two can take them for walks with Mrs Finlay and Trigger. Come on now, your dad has something to show you.'

Trigger was the Finlays' new dog and the Grindlewood residents had already heard about him. They knew his bark and the birds had flown over to the farm to see him. He was a clever and friendly black-and-white border collie and would make a great addition to their team. They liked the idea of another dog being around, even if he was living over on the farm.

In the yard, Greg showed off another wooden shelter he had built. This time it was a really big one for the swans. He decided to set it up on the far side of the pond where there was more space and fewer disturbances for the birds. He hoped the swan shelter might tempt the swans back, and then the ducks would follow too.

The children were pleased. Afterwards the whole family went over to the Finlays' home on Meadowfield Farm for tea and to meet the Finlays' new dog. That would be the start of the children's stay with the Finlays, while Greg and Gloria headed off to attend to some business in the city.

As well as preparing for the ferrets' return, the residents were anxiously watching the skies for any sign of Oberon and Gildevard. They were several days overdue and everyone was worried that they must have run into trouble. Or perhaps Gildevard was the problem. They just had to keep hoping and waiting.

At regular intervals, the garden birds flew further afield, trying to catch a glimpse of the owl and the eagle on their return journey. Gildevard was their only hope. The residents had no alternative plan. If they couldn't decipher Wanda's powerful magic and cast the spell at the wicked warlock, perhaps he really would be unstoppable. They didn't know how much time they had left. They only knew that it couldn't be long.

Chapter Ten

JUST IN TIME

'WHAAAAAATT?' roared Worfeus. 'EMPTY? What do you mean empty?'

The warlock did not like the ferrets' report of an empty plinth. The garden residents had beaten him to the scroll.

But the warlock had learned from some of his earlier mistakes and he had devised a back-up plan. He had sent a couple of magpies to an old war ally of his in the far north with a message. He hoped that this acquaintance might advise him on the whereabouts of the scroll, as he was equally interested in powerful magic.

This acquaintance, for he could not be called a friend, was an evil buzzard who had a very bad reputation. His first reply, some weeks ago, had confirmed what the warlock had expected all along: that the scroll was indeed in Grindlewood garden. His second message had hinted that it might be in the pond. And so this time, Worfeus had sent his ferrets to get it, but their failure enraged him.

'GO BACK TO THAT GARDEN!' he bellowed at the ferrets. 'FIND ME THAT SCROLL or don't come back!'

He dismissed the ferocious five and retreated to his lair, fuming.

The ferrets sneaked into the garden just as it was getting dark. This time they had a proper plan.

Their first target was the foxes' den. The ferrets pounced as the foxes came out to hunt. They had little chance, with three against five. Norville was nearby and rolled up quickly into a spiky ball. He hurled himself at the ferrets, but they were not in the least bit bothered by his prickly spikes. They seemed to have skin like steel. Instead, they pulled at his spikes, unrolled him and bit him all over his face. Then they flipped him over to try to rip his tummy and tiny tail. Norville tried to curl up once again to protect himself, but the ferrets still managed to bite him. All the residents rushed to help when they heard the hedgehog and foxes screeching, and the dogs barking. Cyril flew over to try to spike some of the ferrets with his beak. The smaller birds flew frantically around, dive-bombing above the ferrets' heads, just as the sparrows had taught them. Some birds got too close and were badly hurt as the ferrets jumped high to swipe at them. Despite their weight and bulky size, they struck with lightening speed.

The dogs raced over, too, but the attack happened so quickly that they could only look in horror at the terrible damage done. The three foxes were badly injured and the hedgehog was in a frightful state. The ferrets then headed to the pond.

Some of the bees had ventured out of the hive to see what was causing the uproar. But as they were guarding the scroll, they had to retreat. Balthazar blocked the entrance tightly. No bee was allowed to leave the hive. The cats ran out of the house and followed the dogs, who were chasing after the ferrets.

'Defend Grindlewood with all your might,' roared Timber.

The dogs barked loudly as they flung themselves at the ferrets. The cats leapt in too. It was a ferocious fight. Skin and fur were flying in all directions. There was barking, screeching and snarling coming from all the animals. There was ripping, tearing, scraping and mauling. There were lots of horrible injuries. The pets had to fight like never before. It was going to be difficult for Ernie to get safely out of the pond and reach all the wounded. And all the while the ferrets seemed invincible. They just didn't stop attacking. Dark magic had made them strong. It was looking very grim.

The fight seemed to go on for ages. The pets were beginning to tire, but the ferrets were not. Just when it looked as if all might be lost, Oberon's hooting and tooting could be heard overhead. The high-pitched screech of the golden eagle followed, echoing through the dark. The huge bird of prey swooped down to attack. He ripped into one of the ferrets, killing him instantly. The ferret turned into dust. Gildevard had destroyed the ferret just before it pounced on Dougal.

Oberon zoomed in to catch another ferret in his talons and beak just before the ferret finished off poor Norville. He tore the ferret to shreds and it turned to dust. Gildevard swept around in a tight arc and flew at breakneck speed after another ferret that had cornered

Cindy. The eagle hooked him in his talons, and then threw him to the ground, allowing Timber and Teddy to jump on him and finish him off.

Oberon flew around in circles over the centre of the garden, watching for the next target. There were two ferrets left.

The Brigadier was severely wounded and unable to move. Sylvie was ripped badly on her side but she still tried to chase after the last two ferrets, who had continued towards the pond. The goldfish were hiding in the little square safe in the plinth. This was a difficult place for the ferrets to get at, as they were too large to get in, especially while the statue was lying at such an awkward angle. Ernie was darting about the pond, trying to find a safe escape route. He needed to reach the injured without being caught himself.

The ferrets then turned their attention to the ducks who had flown in to visit the chickens and the rooster earlier. The timing of their visit couldn't have been worse. They were in great danger. They got such a shock they just flapped about, not knowing what to do or where to hide. Some of the younger ones flew up into the trees. Others hopped into Jamie's little rowing boat, which was tied loosely at the edge of the pond. One of the ferrets tried to climb into the boat to get at the ducks, but the more he tried, the more the boat wobbled and slowly moved out onto the water. The ferret gave up and dived into the pond.

The dogs and cats were barking and meowing at the edge of the water. The golden eagle and snowy owl circled above. They watched carefully for the last two ferrets to come closer to the surface so they could swoop down and snatch them with their powerful talons. They circled and circled, screeching and tooting.

Trigger heard the rumpus down the road on Meadowfield Farm. Jamie and Jemima heard his barking and wondered what was up. Arthur was out, but his wife, Alice, was at home – she had fallen asleep watching television. Jamie grabbed his bow and arrows and a torch, and Jemima snatched a sweeping brush from the kitchen. The children slipped out quietly and ran across the yard.

Unlike the last time they had defended their garden, Jamie's arrows were now the real thing, sharp and dangerous. He had been taking lessons at the local archery club and had already won the beginners' first prize – a set of real arrows.

'Come on, Trigger, we have to save Grindlewood,' said Jamie.

Trigger barked and ran like the wind, streaking far ahead of them across the adjoining field to Grindlewood garden. The children followed as quickly as they could. When he got to the gap in the hedge, Trigger waited. The children caught up and followed him into the garden.

Jamie shone the torch around. The children stopped dead. They were shocked by what they saw. There were so many injured animals and birds lying all around. They saw the foxes and hedgehog lying in a heap. The Brigadier and Sylvie were alive but badly injured too. They had collapsed near the fairy house. The other cats and dogs were chasing the last two ferrets back and forth across the garden as the attackers tried to escape. The ferrets darted through the long grass, the torn-up flowerbeds, the bushes and brambles, and all around the garden as the pets pursued them. Trigger dashed after them to help.

The noise of barking, hissing and squawking was incredible. Overhead, the haunting screeches from the birds of prey added to the dreadful din. Jamie roared at Jemima to be heard.

'Jemima, over here!' He pointed to the well, where he ducked down and prepared his bow. Jemima dropped the broom and crouched beside him. She handed him the arrows one after another as quickly as possible. He fired at one of the ferrets as it charged by. He missed.

The other ferret popped up from behind a bush. It turned around and bolted back towards the rowing boat, then tried to get in where some of the ducks were trapped. Jamie took careful aim, trying to ignore Jemima's shouts and screams.

'Get him, Jamie, get him!'

'I have to be careful, Jemima. I only have six arrows,' said Jamie, very tensely.

'There's the other one, there, over there!' cried Jemima.

Jamie carefully took aim again and shot another arrow, but missed again.

'Now I've only four left!' he said, annoyed.

Jamie took aim a third time, but it was very difficult to see in the dark. Jemima tried to be still and stay quiet, holding the torch as steadily as she could, but her hands were shaking. Before long she couldn't stand it any more and she jumped out from behind the well. She grabbed her broom and rushed towards the chasing animals. In that second, Jamie let go his third arrow and this time the shot went right through the ferret's shoulder, pinning it to the side of his rowing boat.

'Yes!' he cheered, loading another one. 'Hey, Jemima, what are you doing?'

'Ahhh! Ahhhh!' she screamed, trying to whack the last ferret as it ran by. Jamie reloaded his bow.

Back at the house, Alice had woken to find the children gone. She went looking for them and Trigger and then heard the terrible noise coming from down the road. In a panic she rang Arthur who was down at his club, and then hurried across the field as fast as she could. Something told her she would find the children in amongst all that noise.

'Did you hit them, Jamie?' cried Jemima.

'I hit one ferret over there, near the boat but that other one has gone into the pond,' yelled Jamie, as he lined up the next arrow. 'Can you see it?' he cried.

Jemima grabbed the torch again. She swung the light around to try to find where the last ferret was hiding. 'No, I can't see it anywhere.'

'Keep looking,' said Jamie. 'I'm going to put another arrow in that other one – just to be sure.'

Jamie ran over to the ferret he had pinned to the

side of his rowing boat. He took careful aim and let the arrow fly. He hit the target squarely, but the ferret still wasn't dead. Before he could reload, Timber and Trigger jumped on the ferret and that was that. It turned to dust.

The little boat rocked from side to side from the impact of the dogs jumping on the ferret. As it did so, the flustered ducks hopped out and swam towards the duck house. They were safe at last. Everyone in the garden knew there was only one ferret left.

'Jamie, Jamie, I think it's down the other end,' cried Jemima, waving the torch at some splashing further down the pond.

Jamie ran to where the statue lay sideways in the water. He paced up and down like a hunter, watching and listening, trying to see the last ferret in the dark. The torchlight wasn't nearly strong enough, but it was all they had while the moon remained behind some clouds. The heron was stabbing at anything that moved in the water, but so far he hadn't hit anything but shadows.

Of the animals, only Timber, Trigger, Teddy and Dougal were able to prowl along the side of the pond. All the others were injured or exhausted.

Cyril hovered low over the pond while Oberon and Gildevard continued to circle overhead. Jamie strode bravely alongside. Surely one of them would catch the last ferocious ferret.

Teddy hissed and the dogs barked loudly. They could hear and smell the last ferret slowly and carefully swimming to the edge of the pond. Jamie was ready with his loaded bow. Jemima was all set with the broom. She pointed the torchlight on the pond. Everyone waited to see or hear the ferret's next move.

Finally, he took his chance. Ferret number five leapt out of the water and darted through the reeds and rushes at the end of the pond, hoping to disappear under the thicker foliage between the pond and the end wall. Jamie gave it his best aim and let the fifth arrow go. He had just enough distance. They heard a scurry and a few squeals, and ran to take a look. The ferret was hit and injured, but still trying to scurry away, the arrow stuck in his rump. Jemima jumped into the bushes and started swooshing with the broom, determined to whack the ferret out into the open. Jamie took aim again and walked slowly towards where Jemima was thrashing.

'I hit it, Jamie, I hit it!' she cried.

'Where is it? I can't see it.'

'Under here somewhere,' said Jemima, whacking at the bushes again. 'I felt it, I'm sure,' she cried.

The moon was still behind the clouds, making it difficult for the children to see clearly, and it was hard to thrash the broom around and hold the torch too. The dogs and Teddy were racing around the children and in and out of the bushes, trying to flush out the enemy.

Jamie kept his arms raised, ready to fire his last arrow.

The ferret made a last and desperate dash for the hedge.

'There, Jamie, there! It's heading for the hedge.'

The pets chased after it. Jamie adjusted his aim but stopped. 'What if I hit one of the dogs or Teddy?' he thought.

'I can't do it, Jemima; I might hit one of ours. They're too close,' cried Jamie.

'Oh no! It's getting away, it's getting away!' cried Jemima.

Jamie took aim, trying to stay confident. He was a prizewinner after all. He could make this last shot count. He could hit the target and not his pets, couldn't he? It was a hard choice to make, even with Ernie the frog standing by to heal the wounded.

Jamie made his decision. His heart pounded furiously in his chest as he let the arrow fly. He watched it as if in slow motion as it hurtled towards the ferret – and the pets. They were so close together, it was impossible to know where the arrow would land.

The two birds of prey were zooming down on the ferret at exactly the same time. Their hooting made the ferret look up for just a second. It was enough to distract him, and the final arrow struck home.

'YES!' cried Jamie. It had been a prizewinner's shot indeed.

The pets leapt on the last and largest ferret as he struggled to escape, with two arrows sticking out of him now. The eagle and owl flew down, talons ready to close on him. The ferret was caught and torn to shreds. The children ran to the spot to see it dissolve into dust.

'Well done, Jamie!' said Jemima and she gave her brother a quick hug. 'You did it, you did it!'

Jamie felt very proud.

At last, the moon came out and shone brightly. Timber barked for Ernie to come out of the pond to save their friends. The frog started with the foxes, all of whom were on their last breaths. He hopped around all the animals and so many of the birds. The children watched with great relief, as the frog healed them all.

'Are you two all right?' called a woman's voice from behind the hedge. Alice had finally made it across the field. 'There's an awful lot of noise in there.'

'We're fine,' said Jamie.

'Yes, fine, Mrs Finlay,' said Jemima.

'What was all that rumpus?' asked Alice.

'There were ferrets in the garden, Mrs Finlay. Trigger must have heard them. He started barking and we followed him here. Everything is OK now,' said Jamie.

Jemima looked at him. 'I think we're in a lot of trouble,' she whispered. Jamie shrugged his shoulders. At least all the ferrets were gone and their pets were safe.

Arthur appeared from out of the yard. When Alice had called him, he had driven to Grindlewood straight away. He had keys for the house and all the gates, including the one to the yard.

'What on earth happened here?'

'Ferrets, Mr Finlay. I shot two of them with my arrows and the animals got the rest,' said Jamie.

'They were so brave,' cried Jemima, 'and Jamie is such a great archer!'

'Good grief! You should have waited for me before running over here in the dark. Alice was terribly worried, and so was I when she called me. Thank goodness you're both all right. Ferrets, you said. Are all the pets all right?' Arthur patted the dogs on the head.

'They're all fine, Mr Finlay. Trigger's fine too,' said Jamie.

Trigger barked.

'And Ernie healed all the injuries. Ernie's the frog, Mr Finlay,' said Jemima.

'Yes, I remember hearing something about him,' said Arthur.

'Woo, woo, woo,' said Timber, as he prepared to howl very loudly.

Jamie and Jemima hoped Arthur wouldn't ask them too many awkward questions.

'Hey, you're a great dog, Timber,' said Arthur. 'And good boy, Trigger. But next time, wait till your master comes home before you go charging off like that, OK?'

Trigger barked again and wagged his tail. The children checked the cats, just to be sure that they were all right. The other animals and birds headed off to their homes. Everyone was fine.

'I'll have to tell your parents what happened here tonight,' said Arthur.

'Just say we were trying to protect all the animals in the garden,' said Jamie. 'That's all we were doing.'

'Yes, but that will sound bad enough, won't it?' said Arthur, wondering how exactly he would explain it.

Both the children looked a bit glum. They were probably in a lot of trouble – again.

'Don't worry,' said Arthur. 'You were both very brave, and I'll make sure your mum and dad know that too. That's a fine bow you have there, Jamie.'

'Thanks, Mr Finlay.'

'It certainly came in handy tonight.'

'So did your kitchen broom. I mean, Jemima used it to whack the ferrets while I took aim with the bow.'

'My, my,' said Arthur, 'you really are the most amazing pair.'

Arthur pointed to the hedge. He could see the children were reluctant to leave, but they had to return to the farmhouse.

'Come on now, it's time to go. We all need our sleep, even the pets.'

The children walked slowly back to the kennels

with Timber and gave him several hugs and pats on the head. Dougal and the Brigadier were already curling up in the kennel, yawning. Jemima kissed Teddy several times before letting him join the other cats in the house.

Everyone had a lot to think about as they tucked up for the night. It had been the most awful attack on the garden ever.

Luckily, Gildevard and Oberon had made it back just in time to help. The garden was safe and that was all that mattered for now. The residents would meet the golden eagle in the morning and then they could begin to work out Wanda's super-spell. Finally, they were making progress on their quest.

Chapter Eleven

SECRETS OF THE SCROLL

After the phone call from Arthur, Greg and Gloria finished their business quickly and headed back to Grindlewood. The blackbirds had been out and about and they spotted the Grindles returning. There was a lot of chatter as the children told their parents what had happened.

'Jamie was amazing! He shot two ferrets with his bow and arrows!' said Jemima.

'Jemima was really brave. She whacked the last ferret with Mrs Finlay's broom!' said Jamie.

'Well, thank goodness everyone is fine,' said Greg, not looking at all pleased.

'That's because of Ernie's magical powers again,' said Jemima. She hoped that her parents would understand, but grown-ups always find it hard to believe in magic.

'Really, Dad,' said Jamie. 'The frog healed all of them.'

'You saw the damage the ferrets caused, didn't you, Mr Finlay?' said Jemima, sensing her parents' doubts.

'Well, there was quite a mess all right, but I didn't see any injuries on the animals, just a few dead birds lying around,' said Arthur.

'But that's because the frog …'

'Now really, children, this was very reckless of you. You should never have come back to our garden without waiting for Arthur to come home first, especially in the dark! These wild adventures will get one or both of you hurt.' Greg understood how much the children loved their pets and all the garden animals and birds, but they were breaking the rules and he had to be firm.

Jamie was about to protest again, but Jemima shook her head. They weren't going to win this one.

'Right then, I think it's time for supper,' said Gloria, wanting to change the subject. Everyone followed her into the kitchen and nothing more was said about the wild adventures.

Now that Gildevard had arrived, it was time to move the scroll out of the busy, buzzing hive. When everyone was ready, Balthazar called his bees to action. Under the Commander Bee's careful instructions the swarm carried the precious scroll over to the fairy house. They placed the special parchment carefully on the floor. The golden eagle swept in, quickly followed by the snowy owl. Everyone was introduced and then Gildevard took charge of the meeting.

'Ah, the secret scroll,' he said, eyeing the parchment closely. 'I must congratulate you all on finding it and protecting it with your lives. You were lucky that the good witch Wanda left so many enchantments to help you. What a clever, clever witch she was.' Gildevard peered down at the scroll and unrolled it carefully with his talons. His eyes widened with excitement as he looked at the beautiful parchment.

'Some of this language is definitely the same as the inscription on the key, which is a good thing, because I know that language well. However, I also see another ancient tongue and some strange symbols mixed in with some other lettering … very strange. Yes, this may take a while.'

The eagle continued muttering and mumbling as he studied the scroll. It wasn't long before Eldric was rolling his eyes. Norville glared at him, terrified he would upset the proud eagle. It was clear that it was going to be a long day and possibly a long night – maybe even a very long few days.

Indeed it was a long wait. It poured with rain for several days, so the Grindles stayed indoors and the golden eagle was able to continue his examination of the scroll in the fairy house, without interruption. For the rest of the unseasonably wet holidays, the children spent a lot of time poring over their books, usually in Jemima's bedroom.

'It's nice to see you again, Abigail,' said Gloria. 'You've been a great influence on Jamie and Jemima. What have you brought with you today?'

'Hello, Mrs Grindle. My granddad gave me these. He said they would be an inspiration to us, whatever that means,' replied Abigail cheerfully.

'Wow, you do have a lot of books today,' said Jemima.

'Some of them look really old. Do we have to read them all?' asked Jamie.

'Excellent,' said Greg. 'You can't go wrong with books. There's nothing dangerous in there! Have fun, you three,' he called as the children hurried upstairs.

They spread the books out on the floor in Jemima's room.

'These look amazing,' said Jemima.

'They were all in Granddad's cellar, the one I told you about. You have to come and see it sometime, though my mum doesn't like me going down there too often. She says it's smelly and damp,' said Abigail.

'What else is in the cellar?' asked Jamie.

'Jamie, we need you to give us a hand and read some of this stuff too,' interrupted Jemima. 'You will, won't you?'

Jamie glared at his bossy little sister, but he knew she was right. After the ferret attack, it was important to know why those vicious animals attacked their garden and who or what had sent them.

'OK, pass me the history book,' said Jamie. 'I want to see if we're mentioned again.' He opened the end of the book where the latest update should be.

'Look at this!' he cried. 'There *is* more about us!'

'Really! Read it Jamie,' said Jemima. Jamie felt very excited, reading about their wild adventures, as his father called them.

The brave residents of Grindlewood, together with the young boy and girl, once again defended their garden from an evil attack.

'Wow,' said Abigail, 'that sounds so cool!'

The ferocious ferrets, born of dark magic in the warlock's cauldron …

'What!' cried Jemima.
'Shhh!' said Abigail.
Jamie continued:

… failed to do their master's bidding: to locate the scroll that contained powerful spells and bring it to the warlock's lair.

'So those ferrets do belong to that nutter,' said Jamie.

'And it mentions dark magic, Jamie, and a cauldron,' said Jemima.

'And a scroll,' said Abigail.

'Yes, what scroll?' said Jemima.

'What cauldron?' said Jamie, wincing at the thought of what might be boiled in a big black pot.

Abigail opened another, smaller book. 'Look here, it says that powerful spells were always written on special parchment, rolled up in – a scroll. Oh!'

'What's the matter?' asked Jamie.

'It's really hard to read. The whole book is very faded and even where you can see the words it seems to be written in really old English, with all sorts of curly twists on the letters. It's really hard to work out what it says.'

'But now we know there's a scroll,' said Jemima.

'Maybe that's what the pets are up to,' said Jamie. 'Maybe they're looking for the scroll and the spells, or em, whatever.'

'What would animals do with a spell, or a scroll?' asked Abigail.

'Exactly. I mean, I'm sure Timber would know what to do,' said Jamie.

'Would he?' asked Abigail, looking at Jemima, who also looked unsure.

'Sure he would,' muttered Jamie.

'Em, well, maybe,' said Jemima softly, not wanting to annoy Jamie. He believed Timber could do almost anything.

'I think the scariest thing is that warlock,' said Abigail.

'He sounded like a madman,' said Jamie, 'someone who probably thinks he's a warlock.'

'Why do you think that?' asked Jemima.

'Well, how many people go around saying they're a warlock?'

'But the history book mentions a warlock, and it says the ferrets came out of his cauldron, and …'

'Why didn't he chase after us, then?' asked Jamie.

'I don't know,' said Abigail, 'but he is mentioned in here, so it must mean something, something not so good …'

'Oooh!' said Jemima, 'I wonder what he's up to, really. I mean, he can't be angry at our pets, can he? And we didn't do anything to annoy him, not on purpose, did we?'

'The warlock, the scroll, the ferrets, dark magic, history books that update themselves – that's a lot of …' said Abigail.

'Magic,' said Jemima. They were quiet for a moment, looking at each other, trying to figure out how everything was connected.

'OK then,' said Jamie. 'I guess we'll have to read them all.' And he picked up one of the books and started to read. The two girls did the same.

Gildevard spent many days trying to decipher the

scroll. It was taking a lot longer than he expected. The spell was very complicated. It was written with so many twists and turns in the language and so many symbols and letters that sometimes made up only part of a word or part of a riddle. The eagle felt he was going in circles.

Eventually, Gildevard and Oberon decided it was time to move out of the fairy house, so they flew the scroll over to the barn during the night. The swans and heron flew with them to try to disguise the scroll from prying eyes, with their large, wide wings. The two birds of prey would be able to examine it better up in the loft, beside their new nests, undisturbed and unwatched by nervous and impatient onlookers.

The residents were anxious about everything, including the butterflies. Everyone was expecting another vision soon but everything seemed to be taking so long – too long. Eldric was pacing up and down, rolling his eyes skyward. Fern and Freya were now doing the same thing. Norville was walking in circles muttering to himself. The birds couldn't stay still and even the blackbirds were arguing. The rabbits were bickering, the cats couldn't sleep, and the dogs were starting to dig holes around the garden.

'Oh dear, what on earth is going on out there?' wondered Gloria, looking out from the kitchen.

'The whole garden does seem rather unsettled,' said Greg. 'Maybe it's something to do with this awful weather we're having. I don't know if we'll have a spring at all, let alone a summer season this year.'

'Yes, perhaps that's it,' said Gloria. 'I don't think I remember a spring so dark and dreary before. It's such a shame.'

Upstairs the children were still reading.

'Hey, look at this!' cried Jamie, standing at the window.

'Huh?' muttered Jemima, deeply absorbed in her own book.

'Seriously, look! Something's going on in the garden again!'

The girls joined Jamie at the window.

'They're back!' cried Jemima. 'The butterflies are back! I wonder if they'll have anything else to tell us.'

'Oh I hope so,' said Abigail enthusiastically. 'I'd like to see it happen this time.'

'It looks like they've something to tell the Brigadier,'

said Jamie. 'Look! The other pets are gathering around him. It's just like when they gather at night. It's … it's like they're planning something. What is it about those butterflies, anyway?'

'I think I may have found a chapter about butterflies in one of these books. I think it's in the smallest one again,' said Abigail, returning to her pile of books on the floor. 'Here it is. Listen to this.'

The Wandeleis often chose butterflies as a way of communicating magic to non-magical beings, but only to those who were considered worthy of such a gift.

'Wow, does that mean we're worthy?' asked Jamie.

'Sure, but, em, worthy of what?' asked Jemima.

'Worthy of magic,' said Abigail, wide-eyed. They were all surprised by this piece of information, and a little nervous. Abigail read on, almost in a whisper.

The granting of such a gift usually comes with the obligation to fulfil a promise or a quest, and one that would not be without sacrifice or danger.

'Crikey! What does that mean?' said Jamie.

'It sounds like we're stuck with it now,' said Jemima, 'whatever this promise or quest thing is.'

'The next bit has been torn out of the book, I'm afraid,' said Abigail.

'Uh oh!' said Jamie and Jemima together.

❧

'Well, I don't know. I just don't know,' said the Brigadier, trotting towards the fairy house. He sat down for a scratch.

'What is it, Brigadier? What did they say?' asked Timber, as he and Teddy sat down beside him.

'Well, the butterflies said the eagle must translate the spell that's written in the scroll. We already know that. Who else could do it? The next bit is that the butterflies must sing it. SING IT! You know they can only speak *after* they have a vision. Well now apparently they can sing too – but when, and how, and for how long, and, and … I just don't know.' The Brigadier looked as uncomfortable and puzzled as he sounded. But there was more. He took a deep breath and continued. 'The most troubling bit is, that, well …'

'Oh do get on with it, Brigadier,' said Eldric.

'They said that for the spell to work, it must be

cast on the very same spot where the final spells from Wanda and Worfeus' duel clashed – somewhere between the fairy house and the pond. Just how do we organise that?' The Brigadier was scratching his ears one after the other in frustration.

'So that's what they meant by that earlier riddle,' said Eldric. 'You remember, "The Glorious One must come to the well".'

'Ah yes, the one you couldn't figure out,' said Norville, teasing him. 'The butterflies had to explain it for us in the end.'

'Yes, the very same one, thank you, Norville,' said Eldric.

'This is going to be very tricky,' said Teddy.

'Isn't the warlock still stuck in the forest?' asked Dougal, bewildered. 'And, um, why would he come here just when we want him to?' As usual, Dougal asked the simple questions so well.

The residents looked around at each other, hoping for answers.

'Aha,' said Timber, realising just how clever Wanda had really been. 'I think Wanda expected that Worfeus might get the better of her in a duel, and so she cursed him to keep him out of the garden long enough for us to decipher the spell she wrote on the scroll. She knew that someone else might have to finish the quest for her.'

'Very likely, Timber,' said Oberon. 'The Wandeleis never used magic to do anything truly evil; they only used it in defence or for good and kind purposes.'

'We also know Worfeus intends to come here as soon as he can escape the forest,' said Eldric. 'The problem is going to be having the spell deciphered by the time he arrives.'

'Yes,' said Timber quietly, 'but I wonder what else could be in the scroll.'

'Oh I do hope we don't let Wanda down,' said the Brigadier.

Everyone shuddered. The thought of the vengeful warlock arriving before they were ready was truly horrifying.

'We must tell Oberon and Gildevard about this,' said Timber.

Waldorf nodded and he and Wendy flew off to the barn with the news.

'How are we going to do it?' asked Sylvie. 'There are so many things we have to get absolutely perfectly right in order to finish the quest.'

'Don't forget the butterflies,' said Balthazar. 'If they are the only ones who can chant the spell, then they must be protected at all times, but how? They are so delicate, so unpredictable.'

'And so enchanted,' said Serena Swan.

'Hopefully Wanda will have thought of that too,' said Teddy.

The quest was becoming more and more complicated. With every bit of progress came more puzzles and more problems. They were all thinking about what to do next, when the frog started hopping up and down.

'I have an idea!' cried Ernie.

Chapter Twelve

FINAL PREPARATIONS

Waldorf and Wendy arrived at the window of the loft and peered in.

'Coo-coo, coo-coo,' called Waldorf.

'I prefer not to be disturbed. I even asked the barn owl to move out. What is it?' snapped Gildevard.

'Excuse us, Gildevard and Oberon. We have received another message from the butterflies,' said Waldorf.

'Oooh! Well?' Gildevard turned to look at the messengers.

'They confirmed that you must decipher the spell. They also said that all three butterflies must cast the spell on Worfeus, on the same spot where the final spells of the deadly duel collided – somewhere between the fairy house and the pond,' explained the wood pigeon. Oberon looked at Gildevard. This was very precise indeed.

'Fascinating,' the eagle whispered, 'quite fascinating. Thank you. You may go.' Gildevard waved his wing to dismiss the wood pigeons and turned to Oberon.

'This is beginning to make more sense now. The fact that all three of them must sing it is very clever. It would suggest that these symbols here, and that squiggle over on that page must mean that ...' His voice trailed off to a low mutter as he bent over the parchment once again, deeply absorbed in its riddles and puzzles and ancient magic.

Outside, Ernie's latest idea was that the butterflies should move into the statue's trumpet. Everyone thought this was very smart and the butterflies were happy to do so. It was right beside where they usually slept before they had their visions and, being such an awkward shape, it would also provide good protection. The butterflies moved in without delay.

Despite all the worries about Worfeus, there was a lot of chirping and birdsong in the garden during April. Many of the birds had nests full of demanding new chicks and they were busy darting around the garden looking for food. The bees were in full buzz again, the trees were budding and Cyril had returned to the garden after his stay on Lindon Lake. The heron built a huge new nest right at the top of a tall tree overhanging the pond.

But any normality was quickly forgotten when the residents gathered for their meetings. They had many difficult things to discuss. And as soon as the scroll was mentioned, everyone became irritable again.

'We have very nearly deciphered the entire spell,' said Oberon proudly.

'Nearly?' asked Eldric.

'How long is nearly?' asked Dougal.

'He said *very* nearly,' snapped Gildevard.

'And what does *that* mean?' barked Eldric, narrowing his eyes.

'Well, you see …' began Oberon, but Gildevard interrupted.

'Some of the symbols appear to have more than one meaning, so in one case the symbol could mean one thing and in another case the same symbol could mean something else altogether. It is very complicated.'

'You mean the butterflies will have to say one thing, and if it doesn't work, try the other one?' asked Norville.

'That's ridiculous!' barked Eldric.

'Don't be silly,' snapped Gildevard.

'Can't you be more certain?' asked Timber.

'Wanda chose *three* butterflies to chant this spell,' Gildevard replied. 'I must make sure that I put them in the correct order.'

'You mean we have three attempts to get it right?' asked Dougal.

'No, no, of course not!' squawked Gildevard. 'I mean they each must chant part of the spell, one after another. We have to figure out who should sing first, second and third, that's all.'

'You're kidding!' said Freya.

The eagle glared at her. 'We will only get one chance to cast this spell. If we rush our work and get it wrong, the spell won't take effect and Worfeus will be unstoppable. The whole point is to destroy him for good.' Both the owl and the eagle were ruffling their feathers. 'Oberon and I should get back to work. We thought you would like to know that we are making progress, but it will take more time.'

'Yes, we'll keep at it,' added Oberon, eyeing the residents. He understood just how anxious they were.

'Unfortunately,' said Gildevard, 'each butterfly will need to learn the entire spell, just in case we can't

figure out who should go first, second and third until the very last minute.'

'You mean, when Worfeus arrives?' said Teddy.

'What!' barked Eldric.

'That's a bit late, isn't it? You're hoping to get the spell right just as the warlock marches in to destroy Grindlewood?' said Norville.

'I'm working on it as fast as I can. As I said, a mistake would be disastrous,' said the golden eagle.

Oberon shuffled forward.

'The spell is written in very unusual language and the butterflies will need to say all the words absolutely perfectly. I will be giving them lessons every day, starting today,' said Oberon as reassuringly as he could.

But as the butterflies couldn't speak very often, and the ancient witch languages were so complicated, the lessons were bound to be difficult. The butterflies would have to remember the spell in their heads. Many of the residents wondered if the butterflies would be able to do it at all, even if they had been enchanted.

Unfortunately, there was yet another puzzle to solve: the timing of the chant. According to the vision, it must be very precise. The butterflies would have to be sleeping on the statue, wake up at the right time

– with a vision so that they could speak and sing – remember the spell perfectly, chant it correctly, and all the while remain in mortal danger from Worfeus. It was a lot to ask. And their enemy was a most clever and devious warlock, who was determined to stop the garden residents from casting the spell, the only spell that could destroy him. Could they really do it?

Chapter Thirteen

ANCIENT MAGIC

The brightness and cheer of the early days of May were dampened by more awful weather. Dark clouds sat over the forest all day, every day, often extending as far as the garden. The largest clouds rolled into each other with a bump and a bang, finally parking over the spot where Worfeus was experimenting with dark magic, brewing his potions and chanting his spells.

The forest continued to decay. The back field had started to wither too. The darkness was spreading towards the garden, laying a pathway for the wicked warlock.

Bryony kept Gildevard and Oberon fed as they worked on the spell. Having their food delivered meant they wouldn't lose any time, time to concentrate on the translation. More than anyone else, the learned eagle understood just how very clever and powerful Wanda's spell would be. He also knew that in the wrong hands, the crystal key could be very dangerous. He knew it must be magically connected to the scroll in some way, as both items had belonged to Wanda, and he wondered if perhaps it wasn't meant only to unlock the door in the plinth. Perhaps it was meant to do more.

Gildevard knew that each guardian of the key would have enchanted it with more magic, increasing its power and special qualities. Wanda was the last guardian of the key and he wondered who was destined to be next. If no one claimed it, then perhaps it would be his. The golden eagle wasn't about to share any of these thoughts with the residents. His knowledge was his greatest gift and he guarded it carefully. He never told anyone anything that he didn't have to.

But the golden eagle was frustrated that he couldn't decipher the scroll as quickly as he would have liked. After another failed attempt at unravelling the final puzzle, he decided he needed to see the key again. He wanted to compare the inscriptions on the key and on the parchment one more time. But Jemima had started to carry it around with her and now it was usually in her pocket or on a chain around her neck.

'I'll simply have to ask her for it,' said Timber, late one afternoon.

'Right,' said Dougal. 'How will you do that?'

'I'm not sure,' said Timber. 'Jamie wants to do some talking lessons when he comes home from school, so I'll try to think of something by then.'

'Good,' said Sylvie. 'Otherwise it could be ages before we can get it.'

'Let's hope she understands you, Timber,' said the Brigadier.

Timber gave a soft low growl, more like a little groan. He hoped so too.

When Jamie came out to the garden after school, Timber had to try to get his message across.

'Timber, sit,' said Jamie. They always started the lessons with a few easy commands. 'Give the paw,' said Jamie, and Timber obeyed. 'Other paw,' said Jamie. Timber obeyed again. 'Good boy,' said Jamie and gave him a treat.

Jamie had made a list of all the things he wanted to teach his dog. So after the easy bits, he tried to make Timber growl, bark or scrape his paws on the ground for different types of danger. But it wasn't nearly as straightforward as it looked in Jamie's notebook.

Timber understood everything Jamie said, but the real problem was getting Jamie, or any human, to understand the dog. Guesswork wouldn't be good enough for things as important as the key, the scroll, or any part of the quest.

'Oh this is not working, is it, my Super-mal?' asked Jamie wearily.

Timber responded with a few licks on Jamie's hands.

Jamie decided to take a break and he headed for the tree swing at the end of the garden. He began scribbling in his notebook again, trying to come up with better ideas for the lessons. Timber trotted over to the kennel where Dougal and the Brigadier were waiting.

'How did the lessons go?' asked the Brigadier.

'After the easy stuff, not so good,' said Timber, disappointed.

'Not to worry,' said Dougal. 'Jamie is good at understanding what's really important.'

'So far,' said Timber, 'but I'm worried that as we get closer to the end of this quest, we may need to ask the children for help. If Gildevard can't finish deciphering the spell, the only other place I can think of where we might get help is in the children's books. If only we could read.'

'Wow, that would be amazing!' said Dougal.

Jemima and Abigail came out of the house, very excited.

'Jamie, Jamie!' cried Jemima. 'Just listen to this!'

Abigail was carrying the enormous *History of Magic* book. It was so big and heavy she had to walk slowly.

'Go on, Abigail, you read it out,' said Jemima. The three of them sat down on the patio chairs to listen. The dogs mooched over to listen too. Timber glanced at the other dogs, as if to say, 'See what I mean?'

'It says here that the Wandelei clan had magical treasures. One of these treasures was a crystal key,' Abigail explained, before she started to read from the book:

The Wandelei crystal key is endowed with powerful magic. It has been passed down from one queen to the next for centuries. Each queen of the Wandeleis imparts her own special magic to its crystal heart, thereby increasing its power and capabilities over time. It is a powerful medium of magic that must never fall into the hands of unworthy guardians.

Abigail paused. 'That sounds like your key, Jemima,' she said, almost breathless with excitement.

Even Jamie was listening carefully. 'It sounds like all this is happening right now,' he said, wrinkling his nose.

'Yes, it does,' said Jemima, taking the key out of her pocket. 'It sounds really urgent.' The three children looked at it closely.

The dogs looked at the key, too, and then at each other. They wondered what the children were going to do with it. They had to bring it to Gildevard somehow.

Timber moved closer and put his muzzle against Jamie's knee. This was it, the moment to really use those talking lessons. He growled softly, nudging Jamie with his wet nose. Then he put his big front paw on the key, knocking it on the ground, so he could drag it towards him. Then he stopped, looked at Jamie and barked. He nosed the key again, and barked again. He continued to softly growl and shake his ears, stand up and sit down, again and again.

'Wow, I think Timber is talking. At last!' Jamie said.

'He sure is,' said Abigail, staring at him.

'I think he wants the key,' said Jemima.

'Yep, I think so,' said Jamie confidently. 'I'll ask him. Timber, do you want this key?'

Timber barked. It was definitely his *yes* bark. Then he stood up and wagged his bushy tail.

'That's it, he wants the key. But what could he want it for?' said Jamie.

The children wondered what to do. The girls returned to their book, hoping to somehow find the answer. Timber sat beside them, his two front paws lying on top of the key, as if to hide it. He kept growling softly. Dougal ran inside to call the cats. They quickly followed him outside.

'The key!' whispered Cindy.

'How did you get it?' asked Sylvie, looking from the dogs to the children and back again. The cats approached the children slowly, meowing.

'The cats seem to know what Timber wants,' said Jemima.

'So do Dougal and the Brigadier,' said Jamie. 'Look at them.'

'It seems the talking lessons paid off after all. Ha ha!' barked the Brigadier.

'Excellent!' said Teddy, rubbing his head against his

best friend. 'Well done, Timber!'

'I had better take it over to the fairy house right away,' said Sylvie. 'Do you think the children will let me?'

Timber pushed the key towards Sylvie with his paw as the children watched. He growled softly and looked at them as if to say, 'Don't worry.' The children said nothing at all. They hardly moved. Sylvie picked up the key in her mouth.

The children followed the cat to the fairy house, with the dogs following behind. Dougal and Timber loosened the floorboards with their paws and Sylvie dropped the key into its hiding place. Teddy ran off to the barn to tell the owl and eagle that they had the key.

'Wow, this is amazing,' said Jemima.

'It must be really important to them, if they're hiding it,' said Abigail.

'But what does it open?' asked Jamie, puzzled. 'And how do the pets know?'

No one answered. Timber barked.

'I don't know what that bark means,' said Jamie, disappointed. He rubbed his dog's ears. 'Well done, boy, well done. If you want us to leave the key in here, we will.'

Timber barked again and licked Jamie's hands.

'Yes, of course we will,' said Jemima.

'Hey, look!' said Abigail. 'I've found something here.'

Jamie and Jemima moved closer to look at the book. Abigail pointed to some faded drawings and inscriptions that looked like riddles.

'I think we'll need to look at the riddles book as well,' she said.

'Those little picture things look like a puzzle. Maybe if we could crack the puzzle, we might learn a secret code or something. Cool!' said Jemima.

'I already looked at that riddle book,' said Jamie, 'and it's a nightmare!'

'Look over here,' said Abigail as she turned the page. 'Look at this!'

It was a picture of the crystal key – exactly the same as their key. There was a short chapter about it, but some of the pages were torn and faded and others were missing. There was another chapter about butterflies too. It read:

Once enchanted, butterflies will have wings all the colours of the rainbow. One will be swirled, one spotted and one striped.

'That's just like our butterflies!' shrieked Jemima.

'Yes, it is!' said Abigail.

'Wow, finally these books are telling us something,' said Jamie. 'Well, a few bits and pieces, anyway.'

The children huddled around the little book. More of the secrets of Grindlewood were coming to light, and pieces of the biggest puzzle of all – the quest – were slowly falling into place.

Chapter Fourteen

CHANGING TIMES

Balthazar called a meeting in the fairy house late one evening. No one could remember when anyone but the dogs had called a meeting before and they were curious. They all sat, stood and perched around the crooked little chair where Balthazar had set himself down.

'Well, you must be wondering what this is all about,' he said to his friends. 'I'll get straight to the point. I am, as you know, Balthazar Bee. What you may not know is that I am Balthazar Bee, *The Twenty-second*!'

The residents looked at him, wondering what he meant.

'I am coming to the end of my term as commander in chief of the hive and I expect to be leaving before year end.'

Most of the residents cried out. They had never

heard him talk about leaving before. He seemed to have always been there, buzzing around, being friendly and funny.

'Yes, I know it's a bit of a surprise, but bees don't really live that long, yet somehow in this garden, we live longer than anywhere else. That has always been a mystery. Perhaps it is another of Wanda's wonderful enchantments. Anyway, soon it will be my turn to buzz off! Ha, ha!'

Balthazar could see that he needed to explain a bit more to his surprised friends. 'My ancestors have lived in this garden for many happy years, and I really am the twenty-second Balthazar to live here and command the bees. The next Balthazar will be the twenty-third and he will take over as commander of the hive. He will take my place as soon as I pass on. He has been learning all my duties in the hive, in the garden, Operation Pollination, and of course, our very special quest.'

'But why now?' asked Dougal.

'My time has come, simple as that. I just thought I should give you all some warning, what with all that's going on at the moment. I have had the most wonderful life here in the garden, and knowing all of you has made me so very happy. Soon, I will be joining all my friends in the great hive in the sky.'

Balthazar didn't like to say it but he was feeling a little sad at the thought of leaving Grindlewood. No one really knew what to say. The Brigadier and Timber stepped forward. They sniffed and nudged the big bee.

'We'll miss you, Balthazar.'

'Nonsense,' replied Balthazar. 'You wouldn't have even known I was gone if I hadn't told you! None of the other Balthazars ever told you. Wait until you meet my successor. He is so like me, you will actually think it is me! I'll go and get him now. It is time you were introduced.'

Balthazar flew out the window and returned with his friend. Most bees look alike, but these two Balthazars were absolutely identical in every way; even their personalities were the same. It was like seeing, hearing and talking to double! The younger bee knew all about the quest and he knew everyone by name. It was agreed that he would attend all their meetings from now on, to ensure a smooth handover when the time came for the older Balthazar to leave.

This would be the last Operation Pollination for

the elder Balthazar and he wanted to make it a most successful one. Timber, Teddy, Sylvie and the Brigadier remained behind with the two bees after everyone else had left.

'Are you really not the same Balthazar I met when I first came here?' asked the Brigadier, still finding it hard to believe.

'That's right, Brigadier. My "*bee*decessors" just never mentioned it before!' replied Balthazar. 'Back then, the first bee you met was probably number fourteen or fifteen! We are all so alike it seems like nothing has changed. This has been happening for decades!'

'Well, I am amazed. There I was thinking I'd been talking to the same Balthazar Bee for nearly twenty years!' said the old beagle.

'Em, what happens when the, em, when your time comes?' asked Dougal.

'I haven't quite decided what I will do,' Balthazar said, but something was on his mind.

Timber sensed it. 'You do whatever you think best,' said Timber. The brave dog tried to be cheerful for Balthazar's sake, but he was already feeling the loss of his cheerful little friend.

'Thank you, thank you, I will. Now, we must be off, I have much to tell young Balthazar here, and he still has much to learn. Cheerio!' The two identical bees flew off.

That evening, just after dark, Gildevard flew into the fairy house to examine the key again. He hadn't taken it to the loft just yet, as its brilliant sparkling was distracting him and its power was tempting him. The animals were taking turns on guard duty.

Everything seemed to be annoying the eagle, so much so, that some residents thought he was ill. Deciphering the scroll must have been the most difficult piece of work he had ever done. He flew back to the loft, still muttering to himself, and he wasn't seen for another couple of days.

The residents often gathered around the crystal key, wondering if they should move it somewhere else. They didn't like to leave it in the fairy house for too long. There was always the chance that someone from the big house might take it. They all had different ideas about where to put it, and reaching agreement was difficult. The discussion went on and on. A few minutes had passed before anyone noticed that the key had actually vanished.

'Argh! Where's the key?' screamed Fern.

'WHAT?'

'Huh?'

'Ahhhh!'

The residents scrambled about searching for the key. They were running in circles, bumping into one another and falling over themselves in a panic.

'Where did it go?' barked Dougal.

'Find it, quick!' said Timber.

'But who could have taken it?' asked Teddy.

'Oh, what are we going to say to Gildevard?' moaned the Brigadier.

'Absolutely nothing!' barked Eldric, scratching around. 'We must find it!'

They were all so confused. Where had it gone? They were literally chasing their tails, noses and beaks looking frantically for the key. But it just wasn't there.

❧

The little rogue rabbit ran off with her prize and hid in one of the many dozens of burrows in the field next door to the garden. It was such a pretty thing, this funny sparkly stick, and this little rabbit hadn't got many pretty things – not until today, that is.

While the rest of the residents searched the garden, the foxes and rabbits began to search around the hedges and out into the fields. They asked some of the rabbits they met on the way if they had seen anything, but none of them had spotted their cousin, the little rabbit thief, just yet. She remained in a burrow, deep, deep down, far away from the entrance, where no one would be able to find her or the key unless she wanted them to.

Everyone was afraid to tell Gildevard, as telling Oberon had been bad enough. Luckily Gildevard had refused to leave the loft for days and Oberon came alone to the fairy house to give an update on progress.

'Oh, this is frightful news,' said Oberon. 'How on earth did it happen? You know how important that key is. If Worfeus gets his hands on it, we are done for. Who knows what other magic it holds? And we may still need it to help us decipher the scroll. Oh, this is dreadful!'

Oberon promised to say nothing to Gildevard for the moment. Luckily he managed to avoid the eagle by spending most of his time teaching the butterflies the ancient witch language. The entire spell had to be practised in their heads because they could not speak without a vision, and there had been no visions for a while. Everyone wondered if there would ever be another one.

But luckily a message did come. One afternoon in late May, the butterflies were snoozing on the statue's head, tired out from spell practice.

'Beware the ragged feathered one,' they wittered.

'What on earth is that supposed to mean?' said Norville.

'Oh, that's not very helpful,' said Cindy.

'It's another puzzle,' said Eldric.

'We have too many puzzles,' cried Norville.

'Yes, yes, steady on,' said the Brigadier.

'We're nearly at the end of this quest,' said Timber. 'We must stay calm. Look what happened the last time we all got flustered – we lost the key.'

Those words put an end to any squabbling.

Everyone knew Timber was right, but it was so difficult waiting for the warlock, watching for the butterflies, searching for the key and now they had another strange message. It was all getting too much.

Chapter Fifteen

SHOCKS!

Gildevard finally emerged from the loft looking very scruffy and tired.

'I must leave at once,' he said to the stunned group.

'WHAT! You can't! We need you to help us finish this quest. You … you promised,' said the Brigadier. The dogs and foxes growled. The cats hissed crossly.

'I'm afraid I must go. There is nothing more I can do,' replied Gildevard.

The residents were stunned.

'So you're running out on us,' snarled Eldric. 'You're running away and leaving us at the mercy of Worfeus, without finishing the spell. You're nothing but a coward.'

'Now just a minute,' retorted Gildevard. 'This is your garden and your problem. I came here to help and I have. I cannot do any more, not without consulting my books, and perhaps, one other, eh, acquaintance.'

Gildevard shuffled on his talons.

'You mean there is someone else who knows more about ancient witch languages and spells than you?' asked Sylvie.

Timber was growling louder. He scratched at the ground. It sounded like they might be right back where they started. Oberon was fuming. He had trusted Gildevard completely, and had admired him all his life. The owl suddenly felt betrayed. He turned to face the eagle.

'Have you known all along that we should have asked someone else?'

'NO! I tell you, NO!' shouted Gildevard. 'I *am* the expert. It's just these last few symbols that have me stuck.'

'Just what are you going to do?' growled Timber.

'I think there might be more than one spell written in this scroll.' The eagle winced. He hadn't meant to say that. He continued more carefully. 'Wanda must have been a genius to write something as complicated as this. It's terribly important that I don't … make a mistake.'

'But I thought that's why you are here,' said Dougal. 'You're the expert.'

Gildevard scowled and finally got to the point. 'There is only one rotten, wretched character who might be able to help.'

'Who would that be?' asked Eldric.

'His name is Bodric Buzzard.' Gildevard spat the words out. 'A nasty, lazy, horrible buzzard, a quite disgusting, ugly fellow, who …'

'Wait a minute,' said Timber. 'A buzzard?'

'Yes,' said Gildevard.

'The butterflies warned us about "a ragged, feathered one". They must have been talking about the buzzard.' Everyone nodded in agreement.

'Hmm, did they indeed?' muttered the eagle. 'Well, as I said, I know Bodric from a long time ago. I already know that I must be wary.'

'Then go quickly and find this buzzard. Get us some answers as soon as you can!' Timber was beginning to have doubts about the eagle, doubts about why he had really come to Grindlewood. And how did the eagle even know such a character as Bodric Buzzard? His instincts told him to be wary.

'Yes, yes, quite,' added the Brigadier, looking from Timber to Gildevard and back again, wondering if there would be a fight.

Gildevard nodded slowly, but his eyes still flickered with anger. He never liked being told what to do. 'I will go and find the buzzard, although there is no guarantee he will agree to help.'

'How long will this take?' asked Teddy. The last thing they wanted was more waiting and wondering.

'It's difficult to say,' muttered Gildevard. 'He's a tough bird to bargain with. I will be back as quickly as I can.'

Gildevard had turned to go, when Oberon fluttered in front of him, blocking his exit. 'You're not going anywhere without me. I want to be sure you'll come back!'

'And I'm coming too,' said Bryony. 'It sounds like you might need some help.'

'Good idea,' added Norville. His nose was throbbing with rage.

It was settled; the three birds would visit Gildevard's old enemy and try to persuade him to help decipher the final symbols.

The residents watched as they flew out of the fairy house. There was a lot of arguing as to whether they would return in time, return with the answers they needed, or even return at all.

The search for the crystal key continued. Both Balthazars organised swarms of bees to fly around the bushes and flowerbeds – but they found nothing. The birds flew around inside and outside the garden – nothing. They even went as far as checking other birds' nests around the neighbourhood – not a trace. The animals searched on the ground, sniffing and digging – still nothing. Even the children started looking for the key once Timber had shown them the empty hiding place.

'Who could have taken the key?' asked Jemima wearily.

'No idea,' said Jamie.

'Never mind,' said Abigail. 'The animals will find it.' She was more interested in what she was reading.

Jemima peered over her shoulder to look.

Jamie looked puzzled. 'Surely the key is more important. What have you found now?' he asked.

'Look at this, here in *The History of Grindlewood*, and here in *History of Magic*,' said Abigail, pointing to pages in the two old books.

'I read some of that one,' said Jemima. 'It mentions the key and the butterflies again.'

'Yes, and here's another piece,' and she read:

Sometimes, there is a magical bond between the butterflies' enchantments and the power of a crystal key. This may be necessary depending on the power of the spell or the darkness of the magic involved.

'And there is also something about a super-spell. Look at this, here,' said Abigail, pointing to a particular paragraph.

There are very few witches or wizards who can control dark magic. The same few will occasionally be able to create the super-spell — the only spell that is known to be able to destroy the most evil and powerful of magical beings. Few have managed it and even fewer have lived to see it completed. This type of magic ...

The rest of the page was too faded to make out.

A couple of days later, Ramona was munching on some dock leaves at the end of the garden, when she overheard something. A few young rabbits were bouncing around nearby, hopping in and out of the hedge. They seemed to be gathering in numbers and heading in one direction – into a particularly deep and winding burrow. They were very excited about something.

Straining her ears, Ramona tried to make sense of their babbling. They were talking about a funny sparkly stick. 'Could it be the key?' she wondered. 'But what would rabbits want with a key? Oh, they are being silly.' She decided to sit in the hedge and watch as more and more young rabbits bundled into the burrow. 'They must have it down there,' she thought. 'No wonder we couldn't find it!'

Ramona hopped over to the burrow. In her excitement she forgot just how big she was. She bolted down the little rabbit hole, but got well and truly stuck. Poor Ramona couldn't move. Her head and shoulders were trapped inside, and her big legs and feet were left poking out. No matter how much she wriggled she just seemed to become more stuck. Ramona was so cross. She nudged and twisted about as much as she could, but this didn't help at all. There was nothing to do but stay still and hope someone would come to her rescue.

Later in the afternoon, Abigail and Jemima ran out to the garden to look for Ramona, like they always did after a long reading session. After a while they started to wonder where she could be.

'Don't worry,' said Jemima. 'She can't be far. We'll find her.' She called to the dogs. 'Timber, Dougal, Brigadier, go find Ramona.' They too had been wondering where the big rabbit had gone. She never ran off at that time of day, knowing Abigail might come to visit.

They sniffed around the edges of the garden, trying to find her scent. Dougal picked it up first. He barked and the others joined him. They pawed at the ground as if they wanted to dig under the hedge. The scent told them she was alive, but in trouble. Timber started to bark. Then Jamie ran out to the garden.

'What is it, Timber? Have you found something?' Jamie looked closely at Timber who was growling and wrinkling his nose. He was worried about Ramona. They had to reach her quickly.

'Something's up,' said Jamie. 'He's snarling.'

'We were looking for Ramona,' said Jemima.

'I hope nothing's happened to her,' said Abigail.

Timber turned around and ran to the little gap in the hedge, the one they had gone through before. The children and the other dogs followed.

'Go on, show me the way. Go on,' said Jamie. The three dogs went straight over to a maze of rabbit warrens. Jamie and the girls ran after them. The dogs found Ramona and immediately started digging her out. Slowly Jamie pulled her free. She shook her ears to clear the dust and grit and stretched her legs to relieve the cramping. She was fine.

Timber nudged the big rabbit on the nose.

'I think Timber wants to ask Ramona something,' said Abigail.

'Timber, is it about the key?' asked Jamie. Timber barked loudly and scratched his paw on the ground.

'That's a yes. It's definitely a yes,' cried Jamie.

'Of course!' cried Jemima. 'No wonder there was so much fuss. Ramona must have found the key!'

'Good girl, Ramona!' said Abigail.

'Wait a minute. That paw scratching is also a warning,' said Jamie.

'Why do you say that?' asked Jemima.

'Because I taught Timber to scratch the ground

with his paw if there was trouble. I just don't know how much trouble,' said Jamie. 'Timber, where's the key, show us the key. Good boy!'

Timber turned and barked down the rabbit hole. Ramona jumped out of Abigail's arms and sat at the edge of the warren. Timber barked to call the foxes to help with the burrowing. The dogs were too big to dig down the tunnels. Carefully, and making sure not to get trapped again, Ramona and the three foxes burrowed down into the warren. It took quite a few minutes but there it was – the crystal key. Eldric took it carefully in his mouth and went back to the garden, with Fern and Freya by his side and the Brigadier and Dougal right behind them. Timber and the children followed. The fox took the key into his den and lay down on it. Until they found a safer hideaway, he would remain on guard.

The children still didn't know why the key was important, but the best way to find out was to let the animals keep it and watch them closely. They went back into the house after putting Ramona safely in her hutch to rest.

'Jamie, you take *The History of Grindlewood*. Abigail, you keep reading the small one with the butterflies in it, the one with no name on the front. And I'll …'

'Hold on, bossy boots,' said Jamie, 'we've all read the history book, even though we never seem to get to the end of it. I want to read *The Crypto-Riddles* next. I like the sound of that.'

'Good idea, Jamie,' said Abigail.

'Oh?' said Jemima, a little surprised.

'Yes, there might be something in there to help us understand what the butterflies and the key have to do with spells,' said Abigail. 'There seem to be pages about that missing from all the other books.'

'What I really want to know is what the dogs know. That's the most important thing to me,' said Jamie.

'Well, I'll take the history book, then,' said Jemima. 'There's still a lot more to read in it.'

'And I'll keep reading Granddad's oldest book, the book with no name. Like you said, it seems to be mostly about spells and how to make them work,' said Abigail.

It wasn't long before each of them found something important.

'This little book says that enchanted butterflies are often used to cast the most powerful spells, but that they must do so in the *right order*. Listen.'

To cast the spell in the wrong order will cause the spell to fail.

'That sounds scary!' said Jamie, 'I wonder what kind of spell they mean. Hey, listen to this from *The Crypto-Riddles.*'

The Wandelei witches used complicated codes to protect their spells from those foolish enough to engage in dark magic without exceptional learning and ability. Only the most expert and knowledgable members of the magical clans would be able to understand and unravel the riddles of such a powerful spell. To interfere with such magic would be foolhardy and possibly fatal.

'Wow, that sounds really serious,' said Jemima. 'I found something too, near the beginning of the history book. I don't know how I missed it before.'

The Worfagons continued to persecute the Wandeleis. Each Worfagon leader was worse than the one before. Leadership passed from father to son, generation after generation. The current leader is Worfeus.

'*Current* leader?' said Jamie.

'Oh dear,' said Abigail. 'I'm sure I've heard Granddad mutter that name when he falls asleep in front of the fire. I'll try and ask him when Mum's not around. She doesn't like me asking him questions about magic.'

'Why not?' asked Jamie.

'I don't know,' said Abigail, 'but she gets really cross about it.'

⟡

That same night Gildevard and Oberon returned, but without Bryony. The two birds looked tired and distressed. The residents gathered in the fairy house to hear what had happened.

'Well, how did it go?' barked Eldric, placing the key on the floor. Gildevard coughed and answered slowly.

'We got the information we needed.'

'What does that mean?' asked Norville.

Tears were falling steadily from Oberon's eyes.

'Bryony is dead,' sobbed the owl. 'Bodric Buzzard was surprisingly happy to help us with the symbols, after he and his friends killed poor Bryony.'

'WHAT!' squawked Waldorf. There were gasps of

fright all around the little house.

'How did that happen?' cried Timber.

'Bryony was flying a little behind us and was surrounded by Bodric's ragged army of buzzards and hawks,' said Gildevard. 'They ambushed her.'

Timber and Dougal were breathing heavily, their nostrils were stretching wide. They were so upset. Teddy was hissing loudly.

'Look, Bodric was always a wicked, mean bird, but he has become even nastier than I ever thought possible,' said Gildevard, scowling.

'Just a minute,' said Timber, 'that doesn't sound right. What really happened, Gildevard?' He walked menacingly up to the eagle, not in the least afraid of his dangerous hooked beak and long sharp talons.

'What do you mean?' said the eagle uncomfortably.

'What really happened?' repeated Timber. He looked at Oberon.

'The hawks attacked Bryony, Timber. That was that,' said Oberon.

'But why?' asked Timber. 'There must be more to it than that.'

'All right, all right,' snapped Gildevard. 'Bodric Buzzard is known to have traded magical information with the Worfagons.'

'WHAT?' cried everyone.

'But Worfeus is a Worfagon!' cried Dougal.

'Why didn't you warn us about this earlier?' said Oberon.

'Wait, wait, give me a chance to explain,' said Gildevard. 'Bodric has no loyalty to anyone but himself. He is no friend to Worfeus. He only gives information in return for knowledge about magic, particularly dark magic. He was known over the years to have done favours for anyone, even the most despicable characters, in exchange for lessons in the dark arts.'

'Now we know why you didn't really want to visit him,' said Dougal.

'Yes, you do,' said Gildevard. 'I suspect Bodric got a message from Worfeus asking him to deal with Bryony. Worfeus must have seen her in the forest with the ladybirds, and he wanted her killed in case she had seen something. Or maybe he just wanted to teach everyone in Grindlewood a lesson. I'm sure I saw a couple of Worfeus' magpies in amongst Bodric's hawk army when we were there. Our visit gave Bodric the perfect opportunity to kill Bryony. We couldn't have saved her. We were outnumbered.'

The residents were shocked.

'Oh, this is awful,' said Sylvie.

'I hope Bryony didn't die in vain, Gildevard. What else did you find out?' asked the Brigadier.

'I now know how to decipher the rest of the scroll. It shouldn't take long to figure out which symbol represents which butterfly.'

'So there is dark magic in this spell, then,' said Timber.

'Yes, there is, and that's why we have to be so careful with it,' said the eagle.

'Can you finish the spell now?' asked Eldric.

'Yes, I think so,' said Gildevard.

Everyone was so upset by what had happened to Bryony. They were very quiet for a couple of minutes.

'We'll go to the loft and get working on it straight away,' said Oberon.

'I see you still have the key. I was a bit worried you might have *misplaced* it,' said Gildevard, narrowing his eyes.

'We'll keep it in the loft from now on while we finish working on the scroll,' said Oberon.

'Are you sure you should keep the scroll and the key together?' asked Teddy.

'Once we have figured out the match between the symbols and the butterflies, we can separate them,' said Gildevard. 'I will need to check the inscriptions on the key and compare them again with some of the writing on the scroll. We need to get to work right away. Time is running out.'

'Indeed it is,' said Eldric.

Oberon picked up the key in his talons and the two birds flew directly to the loft.

The rest of the residents thought only of Bryony.

Chapter Sixteen

INTRUDERS IN THE LOFT

The birds looked on from where they perched in the trees and in the loft window as Worfeus made his next attempt to reach the garden. He moved slowly and strangely as if struggling against a hurricane. Then, with screams of annoyance and groans of despair, the warlock was sucked back to the forest as if tied by an elastic band. He landed roughly in a heap, scowling. The green potion clearly wasn't quite right, but he was getting closer to Grindlewood every time he tried to escape the forest. It wouldn't be long before he would reach the garden.

Gildevard and Oberon eventually figured out which butterfly would be the first to chant the spell, but they were still confused by the remaining two symbols.

Something didn't seem quite right. After many exhausting efforts, the two birds took a well-earned break and flew out to hunt. They had stored the scroll and the key safely away, tightly packed into and under their nests. They left the sparrows and blackbirds on lookout. They wouldn't be long. While they were away, however, they had some unexpected visitors.

The dogs were patrolling near the barn when they heard some wild fluttering around the rooftop. Whatever they were, they were grouped closely together, and they were large and black as the night. They zoomed around the roof of the barn and into the loft, ducking in and out of the little square window at the top. The garden birds were outnumbered and unable to stop them. The big black-winged things were flying all over the place, bumping into each other, as there were too many in the confined space of the loft.

The dogs barked loudly in the yard, bringing the Grindles outside.

'Look up there, Greg,' said Gloria, pointing up to the roof of the barn. 'What are those things?'

Greg looked up. It was hard to make them out in the dark. 'Birds of some sort, or maybe bats. Yes, bats, I think,' he said casually.

'What! Oh no,' said Gloria. 'I'm going back inside!'

The dogs were nearly hoarse from barking. The cats came out of the house to take a look and began meowing at all the fluttering. Then the children burst out of the kitchen door, almost knocking their mother down as she tried to go back in.

'You two should be in bed,' Gloria called after them as they ran by.

'We were reading, Mum,' said Jemima.

'What's going on, Dad?' asked Jamie.

'What's going on up there? What are those?' asked Jemima.

'I think they might be bats,' said Greg, 'though I've never seen any that size before. A whole bunch of them flew into the loft. I'll go and check it out.'

'We'll come with you, Dad,' said Jamie quickly.

'Jamie, the key!' whispered Jemima.

'I know,' he whispered back. 'Come on, before we're told to go inside!'

The two children ran around their father and straight over to the barn. As Jamie opened the barn door, the dogs bounded in, but they couldn't get up to reach the loft, where most of the bats were circling. Instead, they jumped and barked around the foot of the loft ladder.

The cats dashed past the children and up the rickety ladder after the bats. There was quite a mess up there. The bats had disturbed a lot of straw and the two large nests had been bumped about. A few bats still remained and were swooping around. Teddy and Cindy jumped at the bats, trying to scare them away. Sylvie went straight to the nests to check on the scroll and the key.

Eventually the remaining bats flew out the window. The children reached the top of the ladder and entered the loft. They looked around in silence. Greg was right behind them and they didn't want to say anything that might tell him what they suspected – that the key had been taken to the loft. They wondered if it was still there, and whether there was anything else important up there too.

'Oh, I see something has been nesting here. Hmm, it must be that big owl I saw flying in and out the other day. I guess he's out hunting tonight,' said Greg, checking around. 'Is that another nest?'

'Em, I guess so,' said Jamie vaguely, hoping his father wouldn't stay long.

'Oh dear, that's in quite a state,' said Greg, looking

at the golden eagle's nest. Although the bats had disturbed the nest, Gildevard himself had made most of the mess. He didn't like living in a loft and was often shuffling about.

'It's probably better if we don't touch anything,' said Jamie. 'The birds mightn't like it.'

'Good thinking, Jamie. We don't want them to abandon their nests because of us. Come on, let's go. The birds might be back any minute and they won't want to find us here,' said Greg as he began to climb down the ladder. The two children looked at each other, knowing they must have another look around later.

'Coming,' called Jamie. He and Jemima took one last glance around, and then followed their father down.

Everyone went back to bed. After a few minutes Jemima crept into Jamie's room. They didn't say a word, just nodded to each other and quietly crept downstairs. They went out through the kitchen, across the yard and into the barn. The squeaky barn door could easily give them away, so they opened it only a tiny bit and squeezed in carefully. Jamie wedged the door open with a brick, so it wouldn't bang. He had also brought his torch with him as turning on the barn light would have alerted their parents.

Timber trotted in quietly behind them and waited at the foot of the ladder. The children patted him on the head and climbed the ladder carefully.

'Whew!' said Jemima. 'I'm glad the bats are gone.'

'Shh! Don't make any noise,' said Jamie. 'We'll be in big trouble if Mum or Dad find us up here in the middle of the night.' The cats were still in the loft, mooching around.

'Those bats weren't normal, Jamie – they were way too big,' said Jemima.

'I know. I've never seen anything like them,' said Jamie.

'It could be dark magic again,' said Jemima in a whisper.

'I sure hope not – not here, so close,' said Jamie, as he watched the cats. They were meowing softly in the corner, rubbing each others' noses.

'The key and the scroll are still here,' said Sylvie.

'What a relief!' said Teddy.

The children knew the cats must be talking, but they would never be able to figure out what all the soft meows meant.

'Jem, we'll never be able to learn cat language, not that we're very good at dog language either,' he said. 'At least the dogs wag their tails, shake their ears or bark. But the cats, wow, they have a very complicated way of talking.'

'I know, Jamie, but I still think only magic can explain how all these different animals can talk to each other. It's the only thing that makes sense. It doesn't happen like this anywhere else, not that I've ever heard of, anyway.'

'Shhh!' said Jamie.

'Stop telling me to shhh!' said Jemima.

'No, really, shhh!' whispered Jamie.

A fluttering noise was coming closer and closer.

'I hope it's not the bats again!' said Jemima, ducking down.

'I don't think so. Look out!'

Gildevard and Oberon soared in through the window, carrying their suppers. The children jumped behind a pile of straw and watched. The birds were surprised to see the cats and upset to hear what had happened.

'Quick, check the nests,' said Gildevard, dropping his evening meal on the floor.

'It's OK, they're still there,' said Teddy. 'We already checked.'

'Oh, thank goodness,' said Oberon.

Gildevard frowned. 'That was foolish. We shouldn't have left like that, without arranging proper protection.'

'Bryony used to hunt for us, you see, but …' explained Oberon to the cats, but he didn't finish the sentence.

'You have visitors,' said Cindy, nodding in the direction of the pile of straw in the corner. The children peeped out. The owl and the eagle stared at them. The cats meowed softly, telling the birds not to worry. Teddy approached the children, then sat down and looked at them. It was his way of telling the children that it was OK too. Jamie and Jemima walked very slowly towards the nests.

'Jamie, I can see the key. It's peeking out from under the owl's nest,' said Jemima. Oberon tooted and moved closer to his thick, twiggy nest.

'Yes, I can just see it sticking out at the side,' said Jamie. 'I wonder what's under the big messy nest?'

'I saw Sylvie poking under it as we came into the loft,' said Jemima. 'There must be something else. You have a look. Watch out for that eagle, though.'

'Thanks,' said Jamie, and walked ever so carefully

towards the eagle's nest.

The two birds of prey watched him closely. The eagle's eyes widened and he leaned his head forward, ready to pounce if need be.

Timber barked down below and Teddy meowed. They were telling the eagle to trust them.

Jamie very cautiously reached under the eagle's nest and slipped his hand into the gap between the splintered boards. He could feel the thick parchment.

'It's a roll of paper, Jem, thick paper,' said Jamie.

'Oh, let me see!' cried Jemima.

'Slowly, quietly,' said Jamie. 'Don't upset the birds – or wake Mum and Dad!'

Jemima bent down to take a look. Jamie shone the torch at the base of the nest. He lifted it up slightly so they could see what was underneath it.

'It must be parchment, Jamie, a scroll of parchment. Witches and wizards wrote on paper like that,' said Jemima.

'Yeah, just like the scroll we read about,' said Jamie, a little surprised.

'Exactly,' said Jemima. 'Oh, this is amazing!'

Gildevard watched them closely. He was worried the children might take the scroll away. He made a few threatening throat noises. Timber barked below in the barn. Teddy meowed back again.

'Do they want us to take it or leave it?' wondered Jamie out loud. He wished he could be sure.

'Em, I don't know. What do you think?' asked Jemima.

'I don't know either,' said Jamie, watching the cats and the birds carefully.

Gildevard squawked and flapped his wings, then settled into his nest. The children stepped back a little.

'OK, I think he wants us to leave,' said Jemima. 'He looks really cross.'

'He's protecting it,' said Jamie. 'I think we should go. Mum and Dad will hear him, if he toots and squawks any louder. Come on. At least we know it's here and it's safe, and so is the key.'

'I wonder what's written on it that's so important,' said Jemima.

The two children climbed carefully and quietly down the ladder. Timber's soft growls, tail wags and licks seemed to confirm that they had done the right thing by leaving the scroll and the key where they were.

The two children returned to the house. But they

didn't go to sleep. They spent most of the night talking about what might be written on the scroll.

'Jamie, it could be a spell,' suggested Jemima. 'Witches wrote spells.'

'Or it could be a map to find treasure, like goblin gold, or something. I'm sure I read about goblin gold in the big history book. Or maybe it was the magic book,' muttered Jamie.

'I wonder if Luke ever found out some of the secrets of Grindlewood. I mean, it might explain why he disappeared,' said Jemima.

'Maybe,' said Jamie.

'He could have gotten into big trouble,' said Jemima.

'We really don't know, Jem. Anything could have happened.'

'Do you think the animals are trying to find him?' asked Jemima.

'Gee, I don't know. So many questions, but somehow, I think all of this stuff – the key, the scroll, the warlock, Luke, whatever the pets are up to – it's got to be all connected somehow,' said Jamie.

'But how?' whispered Jemima.

The two children finally stopped talking. They

were exhausted. It was nearly dawn when they fell
asleep.

⁂

Worfeus had no intention of sleeping. He spent every
minute working on his revolting potions. He had
made another hissing, steaming yellow one to keep
himself constantly awake. He couldn't afford to lose
time napping. He was more determined than ever to
get to the garden and finish this business.

'At last my moment of triumph is almost here.
When I enter that garden I will deal with those
annoying do-gooders. I will take that scroll and have
its secret spells all for myself. Yes, there is more than
one spell written in that scroll, and more than one use
for all the encrypted messages too. Bodric, my evil ally,
has been useful once again. Those silly garden friends
will never unravel all the power of that scroll. NEVER!
NEVER! And I will find the queen's
treasures too – those enchanted little
baubles that Wanda tried to hide from
me. From ME, WORFEUS! Yes, this is
the end of this nonsense. I will not be
challenged ever again! I AM

WORFEUS, THE GREATEST WARLOCK OF ALL TIME AND I AM GOING TO GET WHAT I WANT!'

Worfeus roared to the night, looking madder than ever. He gulped down more of his gloopy green potion, gagging at the revolting taste. Later, he emerged at the edge of the forest, straining and pulling against the curse that held him there. This time, he made it more than a quarter of the way across the back field before being yanked briskly back. He shook himself down and quickly returned to his potions and spells, determined to speed up his progress.

Chapter Seventeen

A TREASURE TROVE

Gildevard was wondering about the bats. Had they really been sent by Worfeus? Or were they simply looking for somewhere to nest? The forest would have been the obvious choice for them, though perhaps not *that* forest. The more he thought about it, the less he believed Worfeus had sent them. What troubled him more was that he and Oberon had been lazy about their security. They were so tired they couldn't think clearly. They had been lucky this time.

But something else was bothering him. Gildevard wanted to reassure the residents. Some of them clearly weren't very pleased with him and he felt it would be wise to renew their trust.

Swirling wind and lashing rain kept everyone indoors or under shelter the next morning. When the sun came out briefly, later in the afternoon, the garden seemed busier than ever. The bees swarmed out to collect the pollen. Waldorf and Wendy were coo-cooing blissfully at the top of the trees. For a little while, it all seemed quite normal. Looking in on the garden, you couldn't tell that a terrible showdown was almost upon them.

The blackbirds and robins were starving and went looking for food. The robins started pecking around the flowerbeds, and then fluttered over to the well, picking off tiny bugs that were running along its curved stone wall. The earlier gusts of wind had dislodged the wooden lid and the birds were keen to fly down to look for food. The blackbirds had the same idea and joined them.

'Come on, let's go down the well. We rarely get the chance with that lid sitting on top. There's bound to be a feast down there waiting for us!' said Binky.

'Don't be scared! It's a dry well, so you won't drown,' said Billy, teasing.

'Is there room for all of us?' asked Ruby.

'Sure there is!' replied Barty, and off he went down the well after his friend Bertram. The other two blackbirds followed and eventually the robins went down too. Sure enough, there were lots of different bugs down there that made a tasty meal.

But that wasn't all they found. Curious little Ruby noticed something odd at the bottom of the well. She pecked and pecked until the others wondered what had caught her eye. Reggie hopped beside her and starting pecking too.

'What is it?' asked Binky.

'I'm not sure,' gasped Ruby. 'I can see something coloured and round. Maybe it's a beetle.' Ruby liked beetles and chasing them was always exciting. Suddenly, there was a sharp *tap, tap.* She had hit something hard. The blackbirds squeezed in to take a closer look. Stuck in the hard clay was a little wooden box, and embedded in its lid were seven coloured stones.

'Wow, look at this!' cried Binky. 'I wonder what's inside!'

The birds spent the next hour or so digging out the little box, straining their beaks to wedge it out of the wall. At last it popped out. Although it was quite muddy, they could see that the box was beautifully decorated. They simply had to open it. Bertram had a very strong beak and he nudged forward to break the lock.

'Wow!' said Reggie.

'Oh my!' said Ruby.

'Another one?' cried Barty and Billy together.

The box contained a key. The robins rushed up out of the well to tell the others what they had found.

'Goodness me, more mysteries!' said the Brigadier.

'Wanda had a lot of secrets,' said Sylvie.

'This could be very important,' said Timber. 'Waldorf, would you please fly up to the loft again?'

Gildevard and Oberon flew to the well immediately. When they arrived, most of the residents had already gathered. Gildevard couldn't fly down to look at the box as his wings were much too wide. Oberon could just about fit with a bit of careful wriggling. He came back up a bit flustered and dirty.

'It's just a simple-looking key,' said Oberon, 'but I think it might be made of gold, goblin gold.'

'Hmm, a simple key doesn't tell us much, does it? But goblin gold, you say?' said the eagle.

'Yes, I think so. I would need to take a better look to be sure. As it was lying at the bottom of the well, so close to the fairy house, do you think it might have belonged to Wanda?' asked Oberon.

'Yes. She seems to have had a very interesting time here,' said the eagle, wrinkling his brow as he thought about it.

'She certainly left us quite a few puzzles,' said Eldric, rolling his eyes.

'And here comes another one,' teased Norville.

Everyone was wondering if there could be another secret lock, or another secret scroll. And what was that about goblins?

After a couple of minutes, Binky popped up out of the well, very excited.

'Guess what?' he screeched.

'WHAT?' roared Eldric, slightly overdoing it. 'Sorry!'

'We managed to dig out some other coloured stuff, a couple of small bits and something larger that is still stuck in the ground. We're almost done. It's a treasure trove!' He chirped with delight and darted back down. Binky's description hadn't explained very much, so the residents waited patiently.

Soon, they heard a roar and a few squawks. The robins flew up to explain.

'We're going to need Ernie. Bertram has buckled his beak.' The blackbird could be heard moaning in pain. Dougal raced over to the pond and returned with Ernie clinging to his collar. Bertram came up, supported on either side by Billy and Barty. Ernie healed him in no time.

'Phew, that's a relief. Thank you, Ernie,' said Bertram.

'You're welcome. What on earth bent your prize beak like that?'

'Well, I tried to peck out a stone that was blocking the *sparkly* thing. Then I hit another really hard piece and my beak just cracked,' he explained.

'Did you say sparkly thing?' asked Cindy.

'Yes, but that's not all. There are four other pieces down there – five including the key. Isn't it amazing?' said Bertram, shaking his newly repaired beak.

'Jewellery, by the sounds of it,' said Gildevard. 'Hmmm.'

'What's jewellery?' asked Dougal.

'Shiny, sparkly stuff that humans wear for some reason,' said the Brigadier. 'They call them necklaces, brooches and eh, rings, yes. Rings are the things they put on their fingers, if I remember correctly.'

Dougal still looked bewildered.

'We've often seen jewellery in magpie nests,' said Waldorf. 'Normal magpies, that is, not the ones that belong to Worfeus. They're always collecting stuff that sparkles.'

'All these items must have been in that box. They probably fell out when the box hit the bottom of the well,' said Gildevard.

'We had better make sure the magpies don't see any of this,' said Timber. 'They'll want to bring it straight to Worfeus.'

'Good thinking, Timber,' said Gildevard. 'We'd better cover the well for now. We can look at it all properly after our meeting.'

Timber and Dougal pushed the lid over the centre of the well.

'Perhaps Wanda just liked jewellery,' said Dougal simply.

'I wonder if the jewellery is enchanted?' said the Brigadier.

Everyone stopped talking for a moment to think about that, and then they all went their separate ways.

Gildevard and Oberon returned to the loft. They looked out and saw the wicked warlock try to cross the field between the forest and the garden. This time, he got halfway. As he stretched and struggled to get nearer and nearer, all the time fighting the pull of the forest, the field was rotting and withering beneath his feet. Half the field was blackened now, while the other half still looked green. The birds looked at each other. Would they really be ready in time?

The residents' meeting later that night was humming with excitement about the treasure. Everyone was keen to get started but Gildevard wanted a private word with Timber before talking to the group.

'What is it, Gildevard? Is there a problem?' asked the malamute.

'I just wanted to ask you about the Grindles. Humans can be troublesome at the best of times, but what about these children? Are you sure they can be trusted? They seem to have some understanding about magic and the garden, but we don't want them messing things up for us right at the crucial moment, do we?'

'Of course not,' said Timber, 'but I trust the children completely. I trust their parents too, though I'm not sure they understand what is at stake. I am doing my best to communicate with the children. They trust me. I'm sure of it.' Timber spoke very confidently but Gildevard still had doubts.

'Try to make sure they don't get in the way.'

'Don't worry, Gildevard, I will,' Timber replied,

looking him straight in the eye. He believed the children could help but he didn't want them getting too close to any danger. He had to consider everything he asked them to do very carefully.

The first item for the meeting was the bats.

'I really don't believe that the bats were part of Worfeus' plan,' said Gildevard. 'They are drawn to dark places like forests, and that forest behind Grindlewood is most certainly dark and dreary, even in summer. Finding no suitable roosting place there, they probably went looking for somewhere else and came across the loft.'

The residents argued back and forth about this, worried about more invasions.

'Please, please, forget about the bats. It's very unlikely that Worfeus will send anyone else to get the scroll. He will come here himself. We know that's what he is aiming to do. That, and that alone, is what we need to prepare for,' said Gildevard firmly.

'I guess we could handle a bat attack should there be one,' muttered the Brigadier in a somewhat weary tone. It was the first time he had sounded so tired.

'They were much bigger than normal, though,' said Sylvie.

'More dark magic,' muttered Norville.

'Perhaps,' said Gildevard. 'But they didn't do any damage, or take anything, so please don't give them another thought.'

'Have you figured out the last two symbols yet?' asked Timber, changing the subject.

'Almost,' said Gildevard. 'Trust me, we are very nearly there.'

'And how are the butterflies' lessons going?' asked Teddy.

'The butterflies will have the spell off by heart very soon,' said the eagle. The owl nodded. Lots of sighs went around. There was nothing more to be said about the scroll or the butterflies. It was making everyone nervous anyway.

Timber changed the subject again to try to lighten the mood. 'Perhaps we should take another look at the treasure.'

The residents chatted about the treasure trove as they moved slowly outside. Timber pushed the lid off the well with his nose and paws, just enough to allow the owl to fit through. Oberon flew down and picked up each piece one by one: the gold key, possibly made from goblin gold; a large round brooch; a man's ring, again made of gold, with a blue stone; a long, sparkly necklace with seven coloured stones; and a dainty tiara.

'How lovely!' whispered Fern.

'I'd like to wear that sparkly thing,' said Freya.

Eldric rolled his eyes.

'I think they are all very pretty,' purred Sylvie, pawing at the brooch.

'That would look lovely on your collar, Sylvie,' said Cindy.

'Yes, it is all very nice,' said one of the Balthazars – it was hard to tell which. 'What about that gold key? The crystal key was very important, what about this one? What about all of it?'

'You're right, Balthazar,' said Timber. 'It must be important, especially if some of it was made by goblins and owned by Wanda.'

'There are no markings at all on this key,' said Gildevard, turning it over with his talons.

Oberon looked a bit puzzled too. 'We can take another look when we are finished with the scroll,' he said.

'Yes. Let's put everything in the box for now and leave them at the bottom of the well,' said Timber.

'Good idea,' said Teddy. 'They were safe there until now.'

Oberon returned the treasure and the box to the bottom of the well, piece by piece. The birds dropped more leaves and moss on top to hide them. In all the excitement, Timber and Dougal forgot to push the lid back over the well to hide Grindlewood's latest secrets. This would turn out to be an unexpected stroke of luck.

A couple of days later, Worfeus had reached the three-quarter mark across the field. He swore and bellowed as he got closer to the garden, before screeching in rage as he was pulled back to the forest. He looked frustrated and exhausted by all his efforts, but he was still as determined as ever.

The birds looked on from a distance, wondering how soon Worfeus would arrive. Timber and Teddy were particularly concerned. School would finish soon for the summer holidays, and the children would be at home much more. Would their quest be over by then?

The forest was growing blacker and bleaker and

the field behind the garden looked completely dead. Arthur and Greg couldn't understand what was making the grass wither and die like that.

'Isn't it strange how the only field to wither and die is the one closest to that forest? That place has looked weird for years now,' said Arthur.

'Yes, something is up. All the birds and animals seem uneasy. The dogs have been very restless lately,' said Greg.

'My Trigger is barking a lot and running around our yard like a mad thing. Something is definitely bothering him. I just wish I knew what it was.'

'If only the dogs could talk, Arthur,' said Greg.

'Yes indeed,' said Arthur. 'I'm sure they would have a lot to tell us.'

Chapter Eighteen

FIRE!

Gildevard and Oberon were so tired that their eyes were almost shut, yet they continued to study the scroll. The key was lying under Oberon's nest, glowing brightly. The two birds were baffled by this glowing and it was was getting brighter too.

Suddenly both birds sensed something was terribly wrong.

'What's that crackling?' squawked Gildevard.

'And what's that smell?' croaked Oberon, starting to cough. Both birds screeched as they realised what it was – the loft was ablaze! A fire had ignited somewhere near the corner and was spreading rapidly through the dry straw and nesting twigs. Thick smoke filled the space very quickly. The birds flapped about, squawking in terror as the smoke stifled them and made it difficult to see their way out.

Outside, Timber was the first to smell the danger.

He woke the other dogs and they began barking furiously. Greg and Gloria ran out into the garden and saw the smoke and flames coming out of the loft window.

'Oh no, the barn's on fire!' screamed Gloria. She ran inside to ring for help while Greg pulled out the garden hose to try to contain the fire even a little. The whole garden was soon awake. The children looked out from Jamie's bedroom window, where once again they had been reading late.

'Jamie, the birds! The scroll! The key!'

'How did this happen?' cried Jamie. 'Come on. We have to go down.'

The two children raced downstairs.

Greg was failing to contain the fire on his own. He was glad to see Arthur arrive quickly with an extra hose. Trigger had started to bark and then Arthur had spotted the flames from the farmhouse. Trigger came with him and he jumped off the farmer's truck and ran straight over to the dogs. The four of them circled the children, barking constantly. There was still no sign of Gildevard and Oberon. The flames looked set to swallow them up.

The two brave birds were determined not to leave

without the scroll and the key, but both were in the thick of the fire. At last, Oberon emerged with the scroll sticking out of his beak. It was burning at both ends and Oberon's head and neck feathers were badly scorched. Hot ash and sparks were shooting out of the loft as he tried to escape to safety.

The dry old parchment was burning very fast, sending out thick and curling orange smoke as the owl struggled to hold on to it. It was burning so intensely, and the smoke coming from it was so thick that poor Oberon was forced to let it go. As it fell to the ground, it burned steadily to a twisted little crust.

The dogs rushed over, desperately trying to save the last little bit of parchment by trampling the flames with their paws. Despite their brave efforts and burning their paws, it was too little, too late. The scroll was gone. Oberon landed awkwardly, whimpering in pain. His beak had nearly melted and his face was blackened and burned.

'I'm so sorry,' he sobbed. 'I tried so hard, but I just couldn't hold it.' Waldorf and Wendy flew with him to the pond to see Ernie. Nothing more could be done about the scroll. It was gone. Everyone looked up, waiting for Gildevard.

Greg, Gloria and Arthur battled the blaze together but it wasn't looking good. The children were instructed to move back, closer to the house, all the while trying to keep the dogs out of danger too. Suddenly, the burning loft collapsed into the barn below in a thunderous roar. Everyone ducked and shielded their eyes to avoid the hot spraying ash and flying splinters of burning wood. The fire was likely to spread to the other barns if it wasn't stopped very soon.

'Look, it's the eagle!' shrieked Jemima, as she turned to look up again.

'I think he's on fire!' cried Jamie.

'No, it's the key, Jamie. He has the key. It's glowing orange.'

The children and the pets followed Gildevard with their eyes as he soared out of the raging fire. He was writhing in pain and jerking his head about. His eyes were bloodshot from all the smoke. His beak and face were scorched and one of his wings had been hit by a piece of flying wood when the loft exploded.

Despite the thickening smoke, several of the residents could see the key in the eagle's talons. It was shining even brighter than the fire behind him. But

Gildevard would not be able to hold the key much longer. It wasn't on fire but it was boiling hot. He had been forced to pluck it out of the flames.

As he flew from the fire, he was hit by a second burst of hot ash. He screamed in pain, dropped the key, and he crash-landed in the yard.

All the garden birds flew in, darting around in the thick swirling smoke trying to find the key. There were sparks from the blaze shooting about everywhere, confusing the search. Now and again, loud squawks and screeches suggested the key had been found, picked up, and dropped again. It was just too hot to hold.

The scramble for the key was causing chaos in the yard. Greg and Arthur were trying to operate the small fire tender attached to the farmer's truck, but it was difficult work. Gloria had taken charge of the hoses, but had to drop them several times to shoo the pets and birds away.

Timber and Dougal broke through the mayhem and ran towards the fallen eagle. They sniffed him out quickly through the smoke. Dougal lifted him up in his mouth and carried him to the pond. Timber returned to Jamie's side.

'Good boy, Timber. Good boy, Dougal,' cried Jamie.

Dougal returned as soon as Ernie had taken care of the eagle. The dogs continued barking at the flames, which crackled and popped as other parts of the barn collapsed in loud creaking roars. The cats retreated a bit but continued to hiss and meow, adding to the din. The noise was deafening.

Fortunately, the scramble for the key moved away from the blaze, over to the patio and then further down the garden, as several residents tried to pick it up but dropped it again. It was still too hot. Oberon rejoined the scuffle once Ernie had sorted him out, so too did Gildevard. There was a steady line of injured residents heading Ernie's way as they burned their paws, feathers or beaks trying to grab hold of the key, or dodge the flying hot sparks.

Eventually, having fallen into a small puddle, the key cooled just enough for one of the sparrows to take it in his beak. But in his excitement, Sparky Sparrow flew straight into two of the blackbirds and it fell out of his mouth. In the darkness and smoke, no one saw exactly where it fell. They had lost it again.

The local fire brigade arrived and got the fire

under control. The fire chief examined the remainder of the barn with Greg, after insisting that everyone else, including the pets, go inside. He wouldn't listen to any protests. Greg was certain that he had switched off and locked up all his equipment in the work shed. He never left any of his work tools in the barn. It was hard to understand how the fire had started. They assumed it must have been some faulty wiring.

After the firemen left, Greg and Arthur tidied up a little but they decided to leave the main clean-up till the morning. It was late and dark, and everyone was tired. Most of the residents had seen the scroll burn to a cinder and they were terribly upset.

'Never mind,' said Gildevard when the animals gathered in the fairy house. 'I think the butterflies know what to say and how to say it. We have to trust them. After all, Wanda chose them for a reason.'

'I hope you're right, Gildevard,' said the Brigadier anxiously.

'And thank you, Timber and Dougal, for coming to my rescue. I could have been squashed by one of those firemen if I you hadn't found me and taken me out of the way.'

'You're welcome,' said Timber. 'Now, everyone, we need to find the key.'

'Yes, let's start the search,' said Gildevard.

Oberon looked very glum.

'Don't worry, Oberon,' said Timber. 'Gildevard thinks the butterflies know the spell off by heart. They'll be able to cast the spell and finish this quest.'

'Yes, but we lost the scroll,' said the owl.

Timber didn't like to hear the owl so worried, and he wanted to believe the eagle. Would Gildevard say the butterflies were ready if they weren't?

After a little while, the smoke had thinned out, making it easier for the residents to retrace their steps and figure out exactly where Sparky had been when he dropped the key. After much to-ing and fro-ing, fluttering and running around, Eldric thought of something.

'I've got it!' They all looked at him.

'Tell us please,' said Timber, not seeing the key anywhere.

'I think it might have fallen down the well. The lid is off it, look!'

'OK, let's check it out,' said Timber.

They trotted over to the well. The lid was slightly off centre, so the key just might have slipped in.

'I'll fly down and see,' said Sparky. He dived down into the well and rummaged around. He seemed to take ages. Finally, he came up. 'Yes, it's there!' he said. 'It must have bounced to one side and slipped under a lot of leaves and clumps of moss. Whew! I'm glad we've found it.'

'Thank goodness!' said the Brigadier.

'I think it might be time to ask the children for some help,' said Timber.

'Yes,' said Eldric, 'I've been thinking the same thing.'

Everyone was so relieved, and so exhausted. It was a weary group of friends that went to bed that night.

Chapter Nineteen

MORE SURPRISES

The worst of the mess in the yard was tidied up by the time the children came home from school. They raced outside to take a look. The dogs were sitting quietly in the kennel, under strict instructions to stay out of the way. The cats had sloped off much earlier, disliking all the noise and disruption.

'Timber, did you find the key last night? The key, Timber, the crystal key?' asked Jamie eagerly.

'We saw the eagle fly out of the loft with it, but we know he dropped it somewhere,' added Jemima.

Timber gave a muffled bark and nuzzled his nose into their hands. That surely meant yes.

'Oh, good!' said Jemima.

But there was something else on Timber's mind. He growled a bit more and pawed at the ground.

'What is it, Timber? Tell me, boy,' said Jamie.

'What could this be, Jamie? Could it be about the

scroll, the one that was in the nest?' whispered Jemima.

'I don't think so, Jem. We saw that burn to cinders.'

'Oh, I wonder what was on it,' said Jemima.

'Show us, Timber,' said Jamie.

Timber woofed and bounded off towards the well. The children followed.

Jamie and Jemima reached the well and peered down. They couldn't really see anything, just loose earth and leaves. Dougal and the Brigadier joined them and they all growled softly. They wondered if the children would take the hint and find the treasure. It would be better if they did and hid it somewhere safe, before someone else found it and took it away. The foxes came out of their den and sat down to watch nearby. The birds looked on silently from the trees.

'I think the whole garden is watching us, Jamie,' said Jemima, looking around.

'I know, I can feel it,' said Jamie, glancing over his shoulder. He leant over the well and looked down. 'I can't see anything from here,' he said.

Timber jumped up, putting his front paws on the wall. He strained his muzzle forward as if he wanted to leap into the well itself.

'Timber's definitely trying to tell us something, isn't he?' said Jemima.

'It must be important. Let's wind that bucket down and see if we can scoop anything up from the bottom,' said Jamie.

Jemima glanced up at the house. Their dad didn't like them going near the well, even though it was fairly shallow and completely dry. Timber continued to growl.

'That must be it,' said Jamie. 'Something is at the bottom of the well. We have to get it.'

Everyone watched as Jamie hitched up the old bucket and wound it down the well. When it finally reached the bottom, Jamie wobbled the rope a little so that the bucket would roll on its side, making it a bit easier to scoop anything off the well floor. He jiggled the rope a bit more, pulling it gently back and forth, collecting some clay and anything else that might be down there. He felt an unexpected weight in the bucket.

He glanced nervously at Jemima and then took a deep breath to steady himself. He hoped neither the rope nor the bucket would break with the weight of the clay and whatever else was in it. He wound the bucket up slowly and steadily till it was almost at the top.

'Jemima, hold the winding handle while I lift the bucket out,' said her brother. 'Be careful! Keep it steady or we might lose whatever's in it.'

'I will, I will,' said Jemima. 'Be careful not to drop that bucket.'

They were both very excited. The dogs were prancing about. When Jamie was sure it was steady, he gave the handle to Jemima and took hold of the bucket himself. It was very heavy. He lifted it carefully out of the well. They poured the contents gently out onto the grass. They weren't disappointed. There amongst all the earth, moss and leaves was the little jewelled box.

'Look at that!' said Jamie, amazed.

'Wow! It must be treasure, maybe magical treasure!' said Jemima.

Jamie carefully opened the box, revealing the five items inside: the key, the ring, the brooch, the tiara and the necklace of coloured stones.

'Oh wow, Jamie, look! It *is* treasure!'

The dogs barked and the foxes growled. Norville rolled into a prickly ball.

'Isn't it fantastic!' cried Jemima. 'I'm not sure if this is a necklace or not. And this tiara is a bit small. Oh, this one looks nice,' she said, examining the brooch. It had many colours that swirled and spun around its centre. She pinned it on her T-shirt.

'What do you think, Jamie? Aren't they lovely?' cried Jemima, trying the ring next.

It was too big for her, so her brother took a look at it.

'This looks like a man's ring, like Dad's signet ring, sort of,' said Jamie.

'Look, it has a tiny sword carved in the centre of the blue stone. It goes light and then dark,' said Jemima.

'Oh, that's kind of weird.' He took it off quickly and put it back in the box. 'I wonder what this gold key is for.'

'Let's bring everything inside and wash them. Wait till I tell Abigail!'

'OK. We can put everything in the fairy house later,' said Jamie.

Timber was glad the children had found the treasures. He was sure they would have more luck figuring out where the items came from and what they were for than any of the animals or birds could. So now the children were involved in the quest. But the scroll! It was lost for ever. He trotted over to the

Brigadier, who was trying to break the news to the butterflies as delicately as he could.

'I'm afraid we lost the scroll in that awful fire last night. Are you quite sure, em, that you know the spell well enough to sing it or chant it without, em, any, em, any problems?'

They all waited for an answer. The butterflies could not speak but they flew up and down a few times, which was their new way of saying yes. 'Oh, thank you, thank you!' said the Brigadier.

'Let's hope they're right,' said Norville under his breath. 'Just how unlucky could we be? Bird attacks, rat attacks, ferocious ferrets, Bryony dead, some sparrows killed and then the mysterious big bats. We lost the key, not once but twice, and a fire destroyed the scroll that contained the only spell to destroy Worfeus. Just how much more can we take and still succeed?' he squeaked.

'Well, when you say it like that, it is rather frightening,' said Eldric, trying not to laugh at his friend.

'Norville, we have to put our trust in Wanda. We've got this far, haven't we?' said Timber calmly.

'The butterflies have never let us down and I'm

sure they won't this time,' added Teddy.

'Yes, yes, of course, but we've had so many troubles, so many puzzles, and time has to be running out,' said Norville, getting flustered.

'Don't worry, my little friend,' said Eldric, 'we'll manage.'

Norville trundled off, trying to talk himself into a better mood. Eldric decided to keep an eye on him and he followed quietly behind.

Jamie and Jemima cleaned the treasure and the little box and took them back to the fairy house. Jamie pretended to be a knight in armour, brandishing his wooden sword while wearing the blue sword-ring on his finger. He was starting to like this strange blue ring. The sword at the centre of the ring was gold, at least in colour, anyway. It seemed to brighten the more he waved his toy sword around. He couldn't understand how it could do that, or if it was just a trick of the light, but he thought it was cool all the same.

Jemima was busy looking at all the other pieces. The necklace had seven different coloured stones, just like the box. They were attached to a delicate chain of silver. She wondered if they were real. The brooch was very unusual too. The dark-red stone in the centre seemed to swirl and spin. It made her feel a bit dizzy as she gazed at it. Around the outside of the brooch were tiny crystals, with four larger ones evenly spaced around the edge.

'They look like the four points of a compass,' said Jamie.

'I think it's pretty,' said Jemima as she tried to figure out which way to wear it. But it was time for supper and they had to put everything away. They pulled up the same loose floorboard as before and placed everything inside.

'Perfect. We've got quite a lot of stuff in here now, don't we?' said Jamie.

'We sure do,' said Jemima, looking very pleased. The two of them headed back to the kitchen.

❦

Jamie and Jemima were so excited by their find that they couldn't sleep a wink.

'Jamie, I've been reading more from that big history book. It says that butterflies were considered very special by the Wandelei people. It said they used them as "messengers or instruments for powerful spells".'

'What do you mean instruments?' asked Jamie.

'Em, I don't know really. I need to read a bit more. Here, listen to this.'

The Wandeleis revered the butterflies of the forest. It was part of their tradition. They used them often as messengers or instruments to foretell good fortune or to warn of imminent danger. They were also important in the casting of complex and dangerous spells.

'Jamie, that might explain why they told us things, and why the animals get so excited when the butterflies fly off that statue. Maybe they're getting instructions or messages from the butterflies too.'

'Well, the butterflies haven't told us anything for ages,' said Jamie, 'and I haven't seen them fly around the garden much either.'

'I know, but maybe they're getting messages now from ancient witches or something,' said Jemima, enthralled.

'I don't know if dead people can do that, even witches, but maybe,' said Jamie.

'The Brigadier seems to follow the butterflies' instructions. We've seen them land on his head. I wonder what they're telling the pets and why they haven't told us anything more.' Jemima frowned. 'I'll ask Abigail about this too. She might think of something we didn't.'

'OK, but let's ask Timber. You never know, he might need our help. I get the feeling something big is going to happen, don't you?' said Jamie, looking slightly uncomfortable.

'Yes, me too. We must be there when it happens, Jamie, whatever it is and whenever it is.'

'Definitely,' said Jamie.

Gildevard called another meeting. He knew everyone was worried now that the scroll was gone, and the conversation went on and on. He was exhausted trying to calm their fears and explain his own thoughts.

'Can't you see how destroying the scroll was the safest thing to do? Now that the butterflies have learned the spell, the scroll isn't needed any more. It was all part of Wanda's plan,' said Gildevard.

Everyone stared at him. They still weren't sure what he meant.

'What do you mean, *destroying the scroll*? Who

destroyed the scroll?' asked Teddy.

'And who started that fire?' asked Norville.

'The key destroyed the scroll. It overheated and PUFF! – it burst into flames, setting the loft on fire and the scroll with it.' His audience wasn't convinced, so the eagle continued. 'The key itself cannot burn, but the useful life of the scroll was at an end once the spell had been learned, so the crystal key set fire to it, keeping its secrets safe for ever.' The residents listened very carefully. 'Burning the scroll ensured that no one else would ever know the spell.'

'Just as well it didn't happen before the butterflies had learned it, then,' said Eldric.

Gildevard frowned at the fox and moved on to his next point. 'I have worked out the order of the chant. Beatrice will be first, then Bethany and lastly Belinda,' he said proudly. He had unravelled that puzzle at last.

'How do you know for sure?' asked Dougal.

'What?' snapped the eagle. He was surprised by the question.

'Are you sure you have them in the right order?' repeated Dougal.

Gildevard looked like he was about to explode.

'I think that's a good question,' added Eldric.

'I suppose what Dougal is really asking,' said Timber calmly, 'is can we trust the information you got from Bodric Buzzard? You said you had a bad history with him. And he killed our friend Bryony.'

'Bodric told me what I needed to know and that should be that!' replied Gildevard curtly. He was not giving anything away about his meeting with the buzzard, a meeting that had been private. Not even Oberon had been allowed to attend.

'You said the key contained very old magic. What else can it do?' asked the Brigadier.

'The older the magic, the more powerful it usually is,' replied Gildevard. 'The key itself seems to know what to do, if you know what I mean. Wanda's enchantment was very clever.' The eagle didn't seem to want to talk about the other powers the key might have. If he knew of them, he kept them secret.

'More riddles, Gildevard?' asked Eldric.

'No, Eldric, no more riddles. Only Wanda really knows what else the key can do. Perhaps time will tell.'

'Hmm,' said Eldric, not totally convinced.

'As the new guardians of the key, we must decide what we will do with it, once this quest is over,' said Timber.

'Yes, of course we will,' replied the eagle. 'We must be very close to the final showdown with Worfeus, now.'

'Just yesterday, Worfeus reached the three-quarter mark across the back field,' said Oberon. 'We saw him from the loft window.'

Everyone shuddered.

'We have to look after the butterflies very carefully,' said Pippa. She had moved into the trumpet with the butterflies to keep them company.

'Yes, my bees are on guard day and night,' said Balthazar. The room fell silent. The residents of Grindlewood were about to rid the world of the most wicked warlock of all time. Could they really succeed?

'We can do this,' said Timber, sensing the doubt in everyone's mind.

'Of course we can,' said Teddy, cheerfully. 'Good luck is on our side.'

'Not good luck, Teddy, pure magic,' purred Sylvie.

A few smiles passed around the group. They continued to chat for a little while and then they went their separate ways. Perhaps they really did have ancient magic on their side. They would soon find out.

Worfeus knew he should have searched Grindlewood garden properly all those years ago, on the day he defeated that annoying little witch. But he hadn't bargained on all of Wanda's clever tricks.

Soon, though, he would return to Grindlewood and do what he should have done the first time he went there: find the scroll and all its secret spells, take the jewels and then destroy the place for ever. Grindlewood had been a source of trouble for his ancestors, too, and now its days were numbered. Worfeus relished the thought. His wait was nearly over.

Chapter Twenty

NEARLY TIME

The final showdown would not be like any of the earlier battles. The chickens agreed to stay in their coop and not to venture out, no matter what happened. The ducks would wait on Lindon Lake until it was all over. Serena and Swinford and another pair of swans would stay close to the swan house on the far side of the pond, just in case they were called upon to help. Cyril would remain high up in his nest. The rest of the garden birds would remain in their nests, but would fly off if things turned really nasty. The goldfish would take refuge in the little safe in the plinth. There was really nowhere safer for them, but Ernie would hide nearer the surface in case he was needed.

The residents knew the butterflies had to be protected until they could finish the spell. The chant must not be interrupted. They also understood that they must not try to kill or even attack Worfeus. They had to let the dark magic of the spell do what it was meant to do: destroy the evil warlock for good.

Pippa was ready to call each butterfly out one at a time to chant their part of the spell. As everyone waited, with little or nothing else to do, their nerves were in tatters. The three enchanted butterflies sat on the statue's head for their morning nap. They seemed to sense that today would be the fateful day.

Worfeus knew it too. He gulped down two buckets of lumpy green potion. He stood up tall and straight, ready to begin his march to the garden. Valerius stood behind him. The dead trees all around the warlock's lair looked worse than ever. Some twisted into knots, others drooped low and touched the ground. There were more ivy vines and tree roots than before, snaking and wriggling their way around the forest floor. They weren't going anywhere, but they seemed excited for their master.

The fog was still wisping around but it was the clouds that gave away this most sinister of moments. Despite the daytime hour, they turned the sky almost black and sank low into the forest, covering the warlock and his goblin servant in the most peculiar-looking blanket.

Finally, it was time. Worfeus lifted his head proudly, wiped away the last drip of green gloop from his chin and stepped confidently forward. Valerius scuttled behind him and they left the forest for Grindlewood. The ominous dark clouds that had sat over the forest travelled with them, growing in width and height like a super-sized evil cloak. Worfeus walked confidently, believing that nothing could possibly go wrong for him now.

The sparrows and wood pigeons spotted them first.

'Worfeus looks very sure of himself, doesn't he?' said Wendy.

'Yes, and it looks like Valerius didn't get enough of that disgusting potion!' said Spindle, wincing at the sight of him.

'He really is so incredibly ugly!' squawked Sparky.

'I think he's stuck somewhere between a goblin and a vole. How horrible!' said Waldorf.

As Worfeus and Valerius arrived at Grindlewood's back wall, the clouds that accompanied them sank right down to the very tops of the garden trees and remained there, waiting.

The ugly, wicked warlock and his grotesque little goblin struggled to get over the wall. Valerius was rarely allowed to drink much of potion. He was usually only permitted to swallow just enough to turn him back to a squashed and ugly goblin, able to carry buckets of potion – plenty of potion – for Worfeus.

It was far from the grand entrance that Worfeus had expected to make. They slowly heaved themselves over the top of the wall and down the other side into the garden. They disappeared again behind some of the bushes. There was a deathly silence. No one dared to breathe for a couple of seconds and nothing moved. There was no wind, no sound and the light was fading further.

'Trust in Wanda,' Timber whispered to the others, sensing their fear.

'And trust in magic,' added Oberon, from his perch on top of the fairy house.

After another moment or two, they heard a strange glugging sound. It was coming from behind the bushes. Worfeus and Valerius had brought some of the green potion with them. No wonder it had been so difficult to get over the wall. They had been trying not to spill it!

After drinking as much as they could bear, they got up and moved slowly through the garden, staying close to the back wall and thick hedging. They walked heavily as if waiting for the invisible drag to come and haul them back to the forest. Clearly the potion was not yet perfect, but Worfeus had run out of patience. He had decided to risk it all rather than wait any longer. His red-rimmed eyes darted left and right, up and down, taking in everything around him.

They passed close to the hive. Worfeus' face twitched and he frowned. He stopped and slowly turned around. His long, hooked nose twitched again. It seemed to grow longer as he sniffed the air. He smelled something sweet.

'Ah ha! How amusing!' he sneered, turning towards the bee hive.

He reached out his bony hand and thrust it into the hive, sensing that it had once held something magical. Balthazar the Twenty-second was ready and waiting. This was it, his final moment of glory. Just as he promised, he would go out with a bang! He ordered the last few elder bees to swarm. They had volunteered to go with him. They smothered the reckless warlock, stinging his hand and arm, eventually covering his neck and face too. Worfeus screamed, raging at his own stupidity. He jumped about like a lunatic, swiping and slapping at the bees. One by one, they fell to their deaths having lost their precious stings, or been swatted by the warlock's flapping hands.

Then it was Balthazar's turn. He came out of the hive, so proud and so brave, looking bigger and bolder than ever. He was ready for his final moment, defending his beloved garden and his friends. He flew up in the air and made a magnificent curling dive. With a roaring buzz, he landed on Worfeus' hooked nose. He looked straight into the evil warlock's eyes.

'This is our garden and we will never surrender to you. Take that, you miserable horror!' Balthazar landed his precious sting right on the tip of the warlock's nose. Worfeus was taken totally by surprise and he howled in pain.

'Ha, ha! I got him! I got him!' cried Balthazar. He fell away from his target, slowly descending through the air into his final sleep. But before the brave and cheerful bee could hit the ground, he was whisked away by a sudden summer breeze, up with his friends, the brave and noble elder bees, up, up and away to the big happy hive in the sky. The residents felt so sad, but it had happened exactly as Balthazar had wished.

The dogs and cats moved further down the garden, following the warlock's every move. It was difficult to resist attacking the two intruders, but they couldn't upset the plan, not now, when they were so close to finishing their quest. Worfeus had to move into the right spot for the butterflies to begin the spell. He was almost there. Oberon and Gildevard watched anxiously.

'Hold your ground! Stay back!' cried Gildevard.

'I can take that goblin, I can take him,' snarled Dougal through gritted teeth.

'I know you can, Dougal,' growled Timber. 'But we must wait for the butterflies. It's our only chance of defeating Worfeus once and for all.'

Worfeus moved passed the hive, still clutching his nose. He grasped at every tree he passed, trying to steady himself as he went. He was finding the journey difficult. There was still a lot of pull from the forest after all. Perhaps he had been in too much of a hurry to enter the garden. But when he was angry, he was often unpredictable and reckless.

The warlock looked even more deformed after the bee attack. Lots of ugly red lumps appeared where he had been stung. There was one especially large, oozing lump on the tip of his nose, courtesy of Balthazar. He stumbled and then roared at Valerius.

'Get over here with that potion, you miserable, ugly lump!'

Valerius hurried after his master and poured another goblet full of smelly green muck. Worfeus guzzled it down, quivering at the vile taste and lumpy texture. He shook his head from side to side to get the last revolting drop down. Valerius took a quick drink, but got a wallop on the back of his head for doing so.

'Don't waste my potion!' the warlock bellowed.

'Master, if I don't drink, I will be sucked back to the forest and unable to pour more for you,' said Valerius carefully.

Worfeus glared at him and began arguing with his servant. And it was just as well. The children were home from school and were coming out to the garden. Abigail was with them. They were going to show their friend the treasure trove in the fairy house.

Worfeus heard them, too, and he grabbed Valerius

by the ear. He dragged him back to the end of the garden, where they hid behind one of the oak trees. He smacked the vole again. 'Good idea! Why don't you go back to the forest and GET ME MORE POTION! You should have brought enough in the first place!'

Valerius was about to protest but thought better of it.

'Oh dear me!' whispered the Brigadier. 'What if Worfeus attacks the children?'

'Stay here,' said Timber. 'I'll try to warn them.'

Timber ran over to the children, but they were too excited to pay attention. Abigail had brought the small book with her, the one with no name. She was chattering loudly all the way in to the fairy house. Jamie and Jemima were listening closely. They ran inside and quickly closed the door.

Timber returned to the cats and dogs and together the pets moved forward, side by side, towards the warlock and the vole. They had to protect the children and the butterflies, so they tried to position themselves between the fairy house and the statue in the pond.

Worfeus peeped out from behind a tree. He needed more potion before he could cast his own destroying spell. That kind of spell would take all his energy. Reaching Grindlewood garden seemed to make the pull of the forest even stronger, and it made him feel weak. Perhaps he really had come too soon.

He staggered out towards the waiting cats and dogs. 'Oh look, it's the hero dog, the brave malamute,' he sneered.

Timber growled at him.

'And where's that slimy little frog, the warty one with the healing kisses. That was a stroke of luck, wasn't it, having a little froggy friend to kiss you all better? I'll bet you didn't think I knew about him. Well, I know everything, because I AM WORFEUS! Do you hear me? I AM WORFEUS, THE SUPREME WARLOCK!'

All the dogs barked and the cats hissed.

Worfeus whipped out his wand and prepared to strike. Suddenly, a huge flock of bats came out of the dark cloud that was sitting on top of the trees all around the garden. They clustered around the warlock. His roaring and waving both attracted and disturbed them. With so many bats fluttering all over the place, Worfeus couldn't see where he was going, and he fell over a lumpy root. He winced and roared as he stubbed his toe, bumped his swollen nose, hobbled forward and spilled the last drop of potion. Raising his wand again, Worfeus was abruptly knocked over backwards with the force of more swirling bats.

'Get out of my way, you fools; WHAT ARE YOU DOING?' he bellowed. 'Bats are supposed to be allies of the dark lords of magic, YOU IDIOTS!'

Worfeus hadn't expected any trouble once he reached the garden. He tried to fire spells at the bats, but there were so many of them, he kept getting knocked over by their tremendously flappy wings. His spells were shooting off everywhere, but they didn't hit their targets. Finally he crawled out from under the bat blizzard, but he struggled to stand up on his bruised feet. He was feeling a strong pull from the forest much sooner than he expected. He was furious.

Valerius looked like he was about to be sucked back to the forest too, having already slipped backwards several times.

'Pick up that bucket and go back to the forest, Valerius! What are you waiting for? THIS IS INTOLERABLE!'

As obediently as ever, the vole allowed himself

to be sucked back to the forest without resisting. Worfeus whirled around, still trying to shake off the bats. He roared at the cats and dogs. 'Give me the scroll and the jewels. Yes, I know they are here. I know that Wanda had some of the queen's treasures. I can even smell them! I tell you, this is your last chance. I command you, bow down before me, the true master of Grindlewood, and GIVE ME THAT SCROLL AND THOSE JEWELS!'

The cats and dogs growled and hissed back at the warlock. They would have to be very brave and keep him distracted while they waited for the butterflies to start. As of yet, they hadn't shown any signs of even waking up. Worfeus was in the garden. What on earth were they waiting for?

The children suddenly ran out of the fairy house. Timber ran over to them, hoping to distract them, but it didn't work.

'Wow, it's so dark,' said Jamie. 'What's going on with this weather?'

'Oh! Look! Who's that?' cried Abigail.

Jamie and Jemima looked to where Abigail was pointing. They all saw Worfeus.

'Is that the guy who shouted at us in the forest?' said Jemima.

'Wow! Is he really a warlock?' asked Jamie. 'Hey, where did all those bats come from?'

'He definitely looks like a warlock,' said Abigail in a whisper. 'I hope the bats don't belong to him too.'

'How do you know what a warlock looks like?' asked Jamie.

'Never mind that now!' said Abigail. 'We must find out more about the butterflies and the spell. Quickly!'

Worfeus tried to stand and cast a spell, but the potion was wearing off and he couldn't muster enough strength. He retreated behind the bushes to hold on to a tree to resist the pull of the forest. The bats returned to the tree tops.

'The warlock looked like he was trying to cast a spell,' said Jemima nervously.

'He's gone behind the bushes, Jem. We should stay behind the well and close to the fairy house, just in case,' said Jamie.

'I hate it when you say "just in case",' said Jemima.

'Timber, are the butterflies about to cast a spell?' asked Jamie.

Timber raised his head and barked loudly. He wagged his tail strongly from side to side. His eyes shone brightly with determination. He pointed his nose at the statue.

'That's a *yes*,' said Jamie.

Timber barked, and then he growled.

'Look, the butterflies are at the edge of the trumpet. Look, there, near the top of the statue!' cried Abigail.

'Quick! What else does the book say?' asked Jemima.

Abigail read another piece:

The order of the chant is vital for the spell to take effect. An incorrect sequence will make the spell unworkable, usually with disastrous consequences.

'Oh, we really must get this right. I mean, *the butterflies must get it right*,' said Jemima.

'Oh, this is crazy!' said Jamie, turning and looking directly at Timber. 'Timber, are you sure you know which one goes first, second and third?' Timber growled, then whined and shook his ears. The big dog wasn't sure that Gildevard had figured it out correctly.

'I don't think he's sure at all,' said Jamie.

Timber whined.

'Oh, that could be very bad,' said Jemima.

'Wait a minute. These butterflies are all coloured like the rainbow,' said Abigail.

'Yes! The other book mentioned that too. It said a trio of enchanted butterflies can cast powerful spells,' said Jemima.

'Yes – a striped one, a swirly one and a spotted one,' said Abigail.

Timber barked and wagged his tail.

Abigail was turning the pages of the book, looking for another passage.

'I remember that bit too,' said Jamie. 'Can you find it in that book?'

'Yes, here it is. Look, this is the order they must chant *any* spell if it is to work.' Abigail showed the page to the others. 'Oh, it's almost too faded to make out.'

Oberon and Gildevard flew over and landed on the well. They looked down at the book. The eagle realised that he had made a terrible mistake.

'Oh no, I think the order might be wrong!' cried Gildevard. 'Did Bodric lie to me? Oh no! NO! NO!'

Chapter Twenty-One

THE BIG MOMENT

The last few minutes waiting for the butterflies to wake up seemed to last an eternity. The residents were so scared, yet there was nothing they could do but wait. The children were leaning on the well wall, frantically flicking through Abigail's old book, hoping to find something else that might help.

'What about the crystal key?' said Jemima suddenly.

'Good idea,' said Abigail. 'It's the only thing mentioned in these books – other than the butterflies and the scroll – that we know is here *and* has to be magical.'

Timber barked and put his front paws on the wall of the well. He pushed the wooden lid with his paws and nose. Dougal picked the bucket up in his mouth and dropped it at Jamie's feet.

'Good boy, Timber. Good boy, Dougal,' said Jamie.

He peered down the well.

'Is it down there too?' asked Abigail. 'You didn't find it with the other treasures.'

'I guess it must be. Look at Timber and Dougal,' said Jamie. 'They really want us to drop the bucket again.' He thought about it for a second. 'Come on, let's do it.'

'Now?' squealed Jemima. 'What about the warlock?'

'He's gone behind the bushes,' cried Jamie. 'Come on, we have to hurry.'

'I hope it's really down there,' said Jemima.

'So do I,' said Abigail nervously.

'What is it, Abigail?' asked Jemima. She was getting nervous too.

'Look here, in the book. It's a picture of a key with a bright glow. It could mean that it's really powerful. We must be very careful.'

'What do you think it can do?' asked Jamie.

'I really don't know,' said Abigail.

Jamie was trying to secure the bucket with some difficulty. It was rather old and rickety. Timber barked up at Oberon.

'Oberon, can you fly down and get the key?' Oberon tooted back. He brushed past the children and flew straight down the well. In a flash he came up with the crystal key in his talons. He dropped it on the ground beside the children.

'Wow, what do we do with it?' asked Jamie.

The owl and the eagle circled overhead, tooting and screeching.

'I don't know,' said Abigail, grabbing the key.

'Look how it glows,' said Jemima, 'just like in the book.'

'It really must be the same one,' said Jamie, amazed.

Seeing the glow getting brighter and brighter, Worfeus realised what the children had found. He wobbled out from the bushes, waving his wand.

'I want that key. Give it to me now. I want it! I WANT IT!' He stumbled forward a few steps. 'Hand it over or I will finish you all off in one fell swoop!' he roared.

As Worfeus lifted his arms to chant another evil spell, the bats swarmed around him again, descending from just about everywhere. Every time the warlock waved his wand, more bats arrived. They clustered around him, landed on him and knocked him over again. It was a second bat blizzard! The warlock was raging.

'Look out! He's coming, and watch out for those bats!' cried Jamie.

'Oh, he's so ugly, so creepy,' said Jemima.

'Watch out, he might fire a spell,' said Abigail. The dogs barked loudly and moved in front of the children. Abigail was still holding the key. It was shining brighter and tingling in her hand. The children huddled closer together, unsure of what to do. Suddenly, the light from the key expanded and glowed even brighter still.

'Quick! Both of you! Hold the key! Hold the key!' cried Abigail. Without asking why, Jamie and Jemima grabbed hold of it. A dazzling light shone from the key, and yet it didn't hurt the children's eyes. The light swelled bigger and bigger, spreading upwards and outwards, surrounding them.

'What's all this?' cried Jamie.

'Wow!' said Abigail, her big green eyes widening.

'Just look at the key,' said Jemima.

The crystal key had grown to ten times its normal size.

'OK, I give in,' muttered Jamie. 'This must be real magic.'

'Wow, at last,' whispered Jemima, 'real magic.'

'Whatever you do, don't let go of the key,' said Abigail.

Valerius arrived back over the wall, slopping potion all over the place as he tried to hurry to his master. Worfeus took a large gulp of the lumpy gloop. He narrowed his eyes in a menacing frown and raised his wand again. Mustering all his strength after drinking more potion, he marched forward and cast a number of spells at the children, but the spells bounced right off the protective light. The power of the key was shielding them completely.

The cats and dogs didn't know what to do, but they leapt up and down, barking and meowing, as Worfeus tried to strike the children again and again. He was growing angrier by the minute. He fired spells in all directions, raging that the children had the key. Then, to make him even more furious, the bats descended a third time, blocking the children from his view and causing him to misfire his spells.

Worfeus then tried to command the bats, but they simply ignored him. It was as if they weren't real at all. Valerius tried to shoo them away but only created more havoc, as the bats became more agitated by the goblin's strange gestures. It was absolute mayhem, but the bats had managed to distract everyone as the butterflies finally woke up.

'Look over there on top of the statue. Look!' cried Jamie. The two girls followed the line of Jamie's outstretched hand. The butterflies rose up from the statue and hovered. The spell was about to begin.

Worfeus, still smothered in bats, was hysterical. He was weeping and roaring because his big moment was going so dreadfully wrong.

Oberon and Gildevard flew over to the statue and perched close to the butterflies. The danger certainly wasn't over yet. Worfeus was still firing off spells at a ridiculous rate from somewhere under a mound of fluttering wings. There was still the risk that those spells could hit one of the residents, especially the butterflies, before they finished their chant.

Bethany and Belinda waited patiently inside the trumpet. Pippa was by their side, ready to call them out in turn. As Beatrice came forward to begin, Worfeus managed to crawl out from under the throng of bats. The potion was beginning to wear off again and he struggled to stay steady on his feet.

'No, no, not that butterfly!' shouted Abigail, hysterically. 'The one with the swirls of colour is first! I'm sure it should be the swirly one!' Abigail shouted as loudly as she could, wondering if she could be heard over all the noise of the fluttering bats, the barking dogs and the ranting warlock.

'The swirly one is Bethany!' cried Jemima. The butterflies had told the children their names the very first day they met.

The residents heard the children's cries and were horrified. The order of the chant must be right. Everyone knew that. The three children huddled around the book, checking it again to be sure. The pages were so faded that the children didn't all agree at first, but Abigail was sure. The swirly coloured butterfly should be the first to chant the spell. The residents looked from the butterflies to Gildevard and Oberon, to Timber and back to the butterflies. What were they to do?

'I'm telling you they've got it wrong. Look!' shrieked Abigail, pointing to the faded pictures in the book.

'What if we're wrong?' said Jemima. 'The pictures aren't very clear.'

'If the order is wrong, the spell won't work,' said Jamie. 'You said so yourself when you read from the history book.'

'I know, I know,' said Abigail, getting flustered. 'But

I'm sure those are swirls of colour on the wings, there. Look again!'

All the animals and birds stared at the children. Who was right?

Beatrice was peeping out of the trumpet, unsure whether to come out or not. Gildevard flew closer to the children. His keen eagle eyes could make out the pictures and he saw the true order of the butterflies. Bodric had lied.

'Good grief! That evil wretch of a buzzard deceived me,' Gildevard grumbled under his breath.

'Why didn't you allow me to speak with that buzzard?' snapped Oberon, hovering beside him. 'Maybe I would have known he was lying. Why did you keep everything so secret?' He looked angrily at Gildevard.

'Forget about the buzzard. We have to fix this problem. Pippa, it's Bethany! Call Bethany out, now, Pippa, NOW!' screeched the eagle. Pippa looked confused. 'Timber, tell them, tell them!' the eagle screeched.

'Oh, my goodness, what will we do?' said the Brigadier, all flustered.

'Timber, what do you think?' asked Dougal.

Timber had to make the decision. Pippa wouldn't call any butterfly out until he gave the command. All three were peeping out of the trumpet, waiting.

Timber looked from one to the other. Did Bethany know the first part of the spell well enough to chant it properly? She had expected to be second, not first. Worfeus was drinking more potion and preparing to strike again.

'I can see it, Timber. It's Bethany. Tell her! Tell her!' roared the eagle.

'It's Bethany! It's Bethany!' cried Jamie and Jemima together.

Timber had to trust his own heart. Bodric Buzzard was the last person he could believe, and whatever about his doubts about the eagle and the real reason he came to Grindlewood, the big dog always trusted the children. He barked the instruction to Pippa and she called Bethany out.

Worfeus had begun firing more spells just as Bethany came out and began her chant. It was a most peculiar sound, not like words or singing at all, just long piercing wailing that didn't make sense – not to the children or the animals anyway.

'What is that?' cried Eldric from under a bush.

'It's an ancient Wandelei language that is used for casting spells,' Oberon shouted back over the noise.

'It sounds like a lot of wailing to me,' said the fox, covering his ears. Norville had rolled into a ball to dull the sound.

Bethany bravely continued her part of the spell despite the danger of being hit. Worfeus screwed up his face, took aim and fired a killing spell.

'CRACK!' He missed. He fired again and again as Bethany continued.

'CRACK! CRACK!'

Bethany was struck down. Her time was over, but she had finished her part of the spell.

Pippa looked at Timber, wondering who was next.

Timber looked at the children.

'It has to be Belinda. Tell Pippa it's Belinda next,' yelled Gildevard over all the noise. Timber waited as the children checked the book. He wanted to hear it from them.

'The spotted one comes after the swirly one!' shouted Abigail.

'That's Belinda!' cried Jemima.

'Timber, it's Belinda next, it's Belinda,' Jamie repeated.

'They're right, I can see it in the book!' cried Gildevard. 'IT'S BELINDA!'

Timber barked to Pippa and she called the brave butterfly out to continue the spell. Once again it was a long searing wail, but much louder than the first part. The children winced at hearing the sounds and stuck their fingers in their ears. Oberon, Gildevard and the sparrows tried to distract Worfeus, even though they might be hit by some of his spells. They had to ensure the whole spell was cast.

The pets tried to distract Worfeus too, while Belinda wailed her way through her piece. One by one the brave residents were wounded, but they kept on coming back at the warlock, dodging the worst spells but getting caught by some others. Ernie hopped around, healing everyone as quickly as he could, at great danger to himself.

Despite the frog's brave efforts, many of the sparrows and bats were lost, caught by Worfeus' blitzing spells. Only Spindle and Sparky managed to spitfire-fly out of the way again and again, until they were utterly exhausted, falling in a heap behind the well.

'Well done, brave sparrows, well done!' cried Jemima.

'Wow, they were amazing,' said Jamie. 'Did you see those dives?'

'They were enchanted by Wanda too,' said Abigail.

'How do you know?' asked Jamie.

'You said it. No bird can fly the way they did, not without magic,' said Abigail.

'Look out!' yelled Jamie.

Some of the warlock's spells were being deflected around the garden. Although the children were protected by the dazzling light pouring out of the crystal key, they screamed and ducked as spells shot past.

Several more spells bounced off the light and flew off around the garden, scorching parts of the lawn, the flowers, bushes and trees. All the while, Belinda continued her part of the spell.

'FLASH! CRACK!'

'Take that, you painted moth, and THAT!' Worfeus yelled hysterically, firing repeatedly at poor Belinda until he hit her. 'And THAAAT!' Worfeus fell over with the force of his triple-spell.

'CRACK! CRACK! CRACK!'

Belinda was gone. Her last words were just a wailing whisper, but that was enough.

Pippa looked back at the final member of the trio. Beatrice, the brave and beautiful striped butterfly, came slowly out of the trumpet. The final part was extremely difficult to listen to. The wailing was just as loud as before, but much more piercing. The children's ears were nearly bursting with pain from the high-pitched, sharp sounds of the ancient witch tongue, and even the dogs had begun howling at the noise.

Eventually one of Worfeus' spells hit her wing and she slipped down the outside of the trumpet, badly wounded but still chanting. The residents were petrified. Would she be able to finish?

Beatrice was really struggling. With each forced breath she became weaker and weaker, gasping out the final words, slowly and painfully, almost disappearing to a crackling whisper. She gave it one last big effort before she too was blitzed by Worfeus' wand.

All three butterflies were dead. Their tiny bodies transformed into stardust, which was lifted up by the summer breeze, and then sprinkled gently into the pond.

Worfeus and Valerius were completely horrified.

The most powerful spell of all time had been cast — on them! A sharp, whistling wind whipped up around them. The dark clouds sitting on the treetops whirled into a funnel and descended into the garden. Worfeus looked around frantically. He dropped his wand, screaming and groaning, unable to stop Wanda's powerful spell from taking effect. Valerius ignored the warlock's cries and looked around for a way to escape. He bolted for the garden wall.

But the warlock and the goblin could not be saved. First, the shrieking funnel of wind engulfed the warlock. He was slowly crushed, writhing in pain and screaming with fury.

'No, no, I will not go. I will not be defeated by, by, BY THIS GARDEN, BY BUTTERFLIES! I am the Supreme Warlock of … AAAAAHHHHHHHHH!'

The children and residents watched as the diabolical Worfeus was reduced to a small heap of dust. A puff of smoke spat up from the pile.

Worfeus the wicked warlock was gone.

Valerius was next. He was struggling to scale the wall. When that failed, he made a desperate dash for the garden hedge. Gildevard and Oberon had been waiting for this moment. He was an easy target for the birds of prey now. They ripped the nasty vole to shreds and dropped him beside his master's remains, adding to the pile of dust.

The whole garden shook as the black clouds and howling wind combined into one again. It whipped up the evil dust piles and sucked them into the ground – down, down, down to Warlock Hell.

Then all was quiet in the garden.

After a few moments, any remaining gloomy clouds lifted and melted away. The whirlwind whistled happily and whipped off into the distance. The bats dispersed and headed off. Their work was also done. The magic light began to soften and fade, and finally it disappeared. The children were released from its protection. As it vanished, the whole garden was showered with golden stardust. Some of it blew away on the breeze, settling all around the garden, the house and the entire neighbourhood. The scorched trees and bushes around the garden were restored. All was well.

The dogs jumped on the children and barked happily. They were hugged to bits. The cats purred loudly and rubbed the children's ankles. Eldric chased his bushy tail, while Norville curled into a ball and rolled around for fun. Ramona bounced around like a mad thing! Eventually they all stopped rushing around and looked at each other.

'We've done it!' cried Jemima.

'You mean, they've done it,' said Jamie. 'Our wonderful brave pets have done it!'

'Don't forget us,' said Oberon, landing on the top of the well.

'They haven't forgotten anyone,' barked Timber. 'You're considered a pet too, you know!' He barked at the children and pointed his nose at Oberon and Gildevard. Then he barked up at all the other birds that were fluttering in the trees.

'You were all terrific!' cried Jamie. 'Make sure they all know that, won't you, Timber? But you were the best, always the best, my Super-mal!' said Jamie proudly, hugging his dog.

Timber woofed back and wagged his bushy tail.

'I wonder what happens now,' said Jemima.

'Everything should be OK now, shouldn't it?' said Jamie.

'Well, I'm not sure,' said Abigail slowly, picking up Worfeus' wand.

'Huh? What do you mean?' asked Jamie. 'Isn't

everything back to normal now? Oh, what do we do with that?' The three of them looked at the wand.

'It can't do any more damage,' said Abigail.

'Throw it as far away as you can, Jamie,' said Jemima.

Jamie took the wand and went to the end of the garden. He threw it as far as he could, over the hedge and out into the field behind. 'That's that, then! It will rot away in no time!' he said, returning to the girls.

'You know, Grindlewood is so special, I don't think it will ever be normal or ordinary,' said Abigail.

'Yes, I think we need to do more reading,' said Jemima.

'Now?' asked Jamie. 'But the warlock's gone!'

'Not now!' said both girls together.

They all laughed.

'What do you mean you don't think Grindlewood will ever be normal?' asked Jamie.

'Well, just look at all the secrets we've discovered so far. I'm sure there are more secrets out there, somewhere, hidden. And I'd like to know more about that key, and what else might have been in the scroll, and why that mad warlock was here. Wouldn't you?'

'Definitely,' said Jemima.

'Well, I guess so,' said Jamie.

'Let's ask my granddad, all of us,' said Abigail. 'Let's go and visit him soon.'

'Good idea!' said Jamie. 'I want to see what he has in that cellar. I bet he has some cool stuff he's forgotten about.'

They chatted about visiting Mr Allnut while the residents congratulated each other. Ernie was nearly finished healing all the injured when he suddenly plonked down.

'Oh, I feel quite dizzy,' he said.

'I'm not surprised,' said Gildevard, landing beside him.

'Oh, I see, yes, of course,' said Oberon, joining them.

'What is it? What's the matter?' asked Timber anxiously.

'The warlock is dead and the garden is saved. The powers that Wanda gave you have served their purpose,' explained Gildevard.

'You mean I won't be able to heal anyone any more?' asked Ernie, looking very sad.

'I think the enchantments may not last much longer,' said Oberon gently.

'What do you mean?' asked Timber.

'Enchantments only last for as long as they are needed, and the quest is at an end,' said Gildevard.

Ernie felt a little disappointed that he would be ordinary again.

'And what about the goldfish?' he asked.

'They probably won't do any more speed-swimming,' said Gildevard.

Thoughts turned to Sylvie and the Brigadier, who had also received something special from Wanda – the gift of long life.

'I'm afraid their age may become more, em, noticeable,' added Gildevard.

The Brigadier and Sylvie were twenty years old. Perhaps it was time for them to take a well-earned rest.

Greg and Arthur looked into the garden from the yard. They had been rebuilding part of the old wall down at the front gate, when they had spotted a few bats flying overhead and decided to check on the children. When they arrived everything seemed fine.

'No trouble here, then,' said Greg. 'They're in the fairy house again, reading more books. Excellent!'

'Yes, that Mr Allnutt seems to have a great

collection of old stuff. Well, the children like it anyway. That's the main thing,' said Arthur.

'Yes, it keeps them out of trouble,' said Greg. 'And they love that history book you gave us too! That rumpus we heard must have been when they saw the bats. Perhaps they got a bit of a fright.'

'Girls don't like bats much,' said Arthur, as the two men returned to their work.

The children were still talking about what had just happened, sitting around the rickety table in the fairy house.

'You know, even though it was scary, I really did enjoy all that magic!' said Abigail with a glint in her eyes.

The three of them stared at the crystal key, which had returned to its normal size once its bright light had faded.

'That wicked warlock guy is gone for good, anyway,' said Jamie.

'Thank goodness,' said Jemima. 'He was really scary.'

'We must look after this key. It's special, magical,' said Abigail.

'We should keep it with the other treasures,

although I'm not sure there's enough room under the floorboards for much more,' said Jamie.

'I think Granddad has a small trunk in his cellar. I'm sure he'll give it to me if I ask him. We could put all the best books and the treasures into it. It has a huge lock and a big old key,' said Abigail.

'Then we must never lose that key, or any of the keys,' said Jemima.

'That'll be three keys, then,' said Jamie. 'We have quite a collection of stuff now, don't we? And I'll bet that history book has updated again.'

'How exciting to be in a history book!' said Jemima.

'Hmm, I was wondering about that,' said Abigail.

'Listen, we have to keep what happened today a secret. No one would believe us if we told them, you know,' said Jamie, thinking of what some of his friends at school might say if he tried to explain it, not to mention their parents.

'What about Mum and Dad?' asked Jemima.

'No way, Jemima,' said Abigail and Jamie together.

'You know what I think of that idea,' said Jamie.

'And my mum goes mad when she finds me reading this stuff. She really hates it,' said Abigail. 'If you tell your parents, they might tell my mum.'

'You're right. I forgot for a minute that your mum doesn't like all this magic stuff,' said Jemima.

'Right, then. It's a secret, just for the three of us, OK?' urged Jamie.

'Right,' said the girls, 'just for us.'

But that wouldn't last for long.

Chapter Twenty-Two

THE END OF THE QUEST

The celebrations in the garden were interrupted by sounds of wild splashing.

'What's that?' said the Brigadier.

'Look, look!' cried Teddy. They all stared as the statue in the pond seemed to come to life! Timber stepped forward, growling.

'What is going on?' whispered Eldric.

'Oh, dear, what's happening now?' squeaked Norville.

'Goodness gracious,' said Serena. She was sitting with other swans at the edge of the pond. Something quite large fell out of the crumbling statue and plonked into the water. It sat up, shaking a mop of curly brown hair and looked around bewildered. It tried to stand up but fell over. SPLASH! It rolled over in the water and pushed itself up.

The young boy was very unsteady on his feet, and he fell over again – another big splash. The children came out of the fairy house just as the boy stood up.

'Hello there,' he spluttered. 'Thanks for getting me out of that statue. I've been stuck in there for ages.'

The dogs barked and the children walked slowly over to the boy.

'I'm Luke,' he croaked, 'Luke Finlay.' He coughed again. He hadn't spoken for such a long time, his throat hurt. He stood in knee-deep water, wondering if it was OK to get out of the pond. He looked at the children, hoping they would say something.

'I'm Jemima. This is my brother Jamie, and my friend Abigail.' The three children stared at Luke.

He stared back.

'Are you really the same Luke Finlay who lived on Meadowfield Farm?' asked Jamie, looking at him curiously.

'That's me,' said Luke.

'Wow!' said Jamie under his breath.

'Gee whizz!' said Jemima.

Abigail was too surprised to speak.

Luke waded carefully out of the pond, still feeling

quite dizzy. Ernie jumped out of the way, his eyes bulging with surprise. He was delighted to see his friend again.

'We've done it, we've done it!' cried the Brigadier. 'We've saved the garden, defeated the warlock and now we've rescued Luke! We've done it all!' He barked and went over to his young friend.

'Hello, Brigadier! Good dog. I've missed you!'

As Luke petted the Brigadier, the children came a bit closer.

'It's OK, I won't bite!' said Luke cheekily.

'Eh, where were you again?' asked Jamie.

'I was in the statue. There was a big clash of spells and I ended up in there. I was in a deep sleep for years, I think, but even when I woke up, I couldn't move or speak. I could see you, though. I tried so hard to talk, but all I could do was splutter through this trumpet!' He held it up to show them.

Jamie, Jemima and Abigail could hardly believe their ears.

'Hello, Sylvie!' said Luke. Sylvie purred loudly and rubbed his ankles.

The Brigadier turned and barked at the other residents. 'Isn't this wonderful? Luke is back! All of

Worfeus' evil spells are broken!'

'Unbelievable!' said Eldric.

'This magic never ends!' squeaked Norville.

Jemima ran off to find her parents. Timber followed, barking and howling his big welcome howl.

Gloria was baffled by Jemima's talk of Luke being in the garden. She called Greg who was still down at the gate. He and Arthur came up to the house at once.

Arthur was overjoyed to see his son. Luke was back, healthy and well if a little bit confused … and confusing.

His mum arrived quickly and smothered Luke with hugs. 'It's unbelievable! It's amazing!' she cried. 'We're so happy to have you back, son. Where were you all this time? Are you all right? Let me look at you!'

'This is hard to explain Mum, Dad, but I was … well, I was actually stuck in there, in that statue,' said Luke rather quietly, pointing to the pond. He wasn't sure if his parents would be able to believe him. He tried to explain a little about a witch and spells and magic, but his parents kept talking over him and barely heard a word he said. When he pointed to the pond, there was nothing there. The statue had crumbled into the water.

'We've missed you so much, son. Thank goodness you're safe,' said Arthur.

'I'm so happy you're home,' said Alice, hugging her son again and again.

Luke looked rather bewildered and decided not to say anything more about magic. Obviously his parents couldn't understand, but he knew they were happy to have him back, and he was glad to be back too.

'Dad, I think this is real magic,' Jemima whispered to her father. 'We saw lots of magic today.'

But Greg just continued smiling at the Finlays' happy faces.

'It's a secret, remember?' Jamie whispered.

'How do we keep this a secret?' said Jemima, pointing at Luke.

'I mean all the other stuff,' said Jamie.

Jamie, Jemima and Abigail fell back behind the others as they all walked towards the house.

'Don't mention all the other stuff – the key, the spells, the warlock. They'll think we're barmy!'

'It's OK, Jamie,' said Abigail.

'Huh? How do we explain all this, not just to Mum and Dad and the Finlays, but to everyone?' said Jamie.

'That's just it,' said Abigail. 'I don't think they can hear what we say when we talk about it.'

'Wow, she's right, Jamie,' said Jemima. 'They didn't hear a single word Luke said. The same thing happened when I spoke to Dad just now.'

'It must be another part of the spell,' said Abigail. 'No one knows any of it. Maybe it's a good thing.'

'I bet it has something to do with all that stardust that blew around when the light disappeared,' said Jemima.

'What? Really?' said Jamie, brushing down his sleeves. 'Well if it means we have less explaining to do, that's good. Hang on – we still know all about it, don't we? I guess that means we're the *only* ones who know. Wow!'

The others didn't say anything. They were thinking about their enormous secret.

They ran on to catch up with the grown-ups and Luke and everyone went inside. The dogs were still barking and jumping around. The cats were following and purring too.

'Let's get you home and into some clean clothes. And you must be starving!' said Alice, still holding her son tight to her. She was almost afraid to let him go.

'Greg, Gloria, you and the children must come over later and celebrate with us. Drop in this afternoon and we'll have a little private party,' said Arthur. 'I'm sure all the children would like to get to know each other.'

'Thanks, Arthur, we'd love to,' said Greg.

The children were very keen to talk to their new friend about the magic and spells they had seen that day. Luke had been at the centre of it right from the start. They were dying to know what else he could tell them.

But they didn't really get a chance during the afternoon party. It was the next day, late in the afternoon, when the children were finally able to talk. Their parents still didn't seem to know anything about what had really happened. They just kept repeating that they were glad Luke was home. Eventually Luke stopped trying to explain anything. He knew that he could talk to his new friends, Jamie, Jemima and Abigail about it, even if his parents couldn't understand.

'I first met Wanda in Grindlewood garden,' said Luke. 'I used to tidy the pond and play with the frog, the Brigadier and Sylvie. But one day I found her getting out of the pond, soaking wet. I thought she had fallen in.' His three new friends hardly moved as they listened to his story. 'I guess she must have decided she could trust me, because she told me her secret.'

'The magic,' said Jemima.

'The warlock,' said Jamie.

'The scroll,' said Abigail.

'Yes, yes and yes,' said Luke. 'Wanda said she had a special scroll of parchment and it was terribly important. She said there was a secret compartment in the bottom of the fountain and that she had put the scroll in there for safe keeping. She made me promise not to tell anyone, and I didn't mind keeping it a secret, so I promised.'

'But why did she make it all so complicated? Our pets have had a really tough time,' said Jamie.

'She said a very powerful spell was written on the parchment and that it would take real courage, kindness and true friendship to first unlock all the secrets of the garden and then to allow all the magic of the spell to work,' replied Luke. 'No one could fulfil the task alone, she said.'

'That sounds heavy,' said Jamie.

'It sounds like something from one of our books,' said Jemima.

'But I guess she didn't want the spell to fall into the wrong hands,' said Abigail. 'The little book said only the brave and the worthy would be able to complete such a special quest.'

'Huh?' said Jamie, staring at Abigail.

Jemima stared at Abigail too.

'Wanda used to speak like that!' said Luke.

'Eh, right, so how did you end up in the statue?' asked Jamie.

'One day I was at the pond and I heard strange noises coming from the end of the garden. I followed the sounds of crackling and fizzing, shouts and screams. I was hoping to try to help but I couldn't see much at first. Then this crazy warlock appeared right in front of me and cast a spell, probably to kill me. Wanda cast a spell at him at the same time. I tried to run, but the two spells seemed to crash together and I remember a bright light and then flying through the air. And then I ended up in the statue.'

'Oh!' said Abigail.

'Wow!' said Jemima.

'Crikey!' said Jamie.

'I fell into a deep sleep for ages and dreamed the whole thing over and over. It must have been Wanda's way of explaining it to me, I guess.'

'That's how she saved you,' said Abigail. 'Her spell stopped the warlock's spell from killing you.'

'It put Luke in the statue, though,' said Jamie.

'I guess it was the best she could do against the

warlock's powerful killing spell,' said Abigail.

The others looked at Abigail again.

'Such amazing magic!' said Jemima.

'When you moved into the big house, everything changed,' said Luke. 'I woke up sometimes and I was really scared, stuck and unable to move. There was nothing I could do but wait for someone to finish Wanda's quest and hopefully free me too.'

'Wanda was so clever,' said Jemima.

'I still think it was all very complicated,' said Jamie.

'That's because she had to use dark magic. Light magic is, well, lighter, simpler,' said Abigail.

'You seem to know a lot,' said Luke.

'The girls have a whole library on magic,' said Jamie.

'Yes, we do, and we've got an extra reader now!' said Jemima, smiling at Luke. All four of them were smiling.

❧

All of the residents who had been enchanted were losing their special powers. Soon, Ernie and the goldfish were content with being normal again. The butterflies were gone, but new ones had appeared in the garden and were happily flitting about. No one knew yet if they were enchanted, but time would tell. The Brigadier and Sylvie looked more their age, but they were happy and well. They liked to sleep a lot more than they used to, but no one seemed to mind.

It was time for Gildevard to leave. Before he flew off, he wanted to have a few words with Oberon and Timber.

'That was a piece of luck, you know, the children understanding *The Book of Enchantments*,' said Gildevard.

'Yes, I thought I recognised the little book. I wonder where they got it. There are very few copies of it nowadays,' said Oberon.

'We could have been in a lot of trouble without it,' said Timber, eyeing the eagle.

'Yes, that dastardly buzzard lied to me and I admit I should have known better. But he was clever about it.'

'What exactly did Bodric say to you, Gildevard? Was there a reason you wouldn't let me listen in on your conversation?' asked Oberon a little crossly.

'That's private, Oberon. Don't worry about it. We succeeded in the end, didn't we? That's all that matters now.'

'And it was very lucky we did,' said Oberon.

'You'll be staying in Grindlewood, then?' asked Gildevard, changing the subject.

'Yes, I will. I feel I belong here now, if the residents will have me,' said the owl.

'We are very happy to have you,' said Timber.

Oberon nodded politely.

'Keep a close eye on things, won't you, Timber?'

'I certainly will, Gildevard,' said Timber. 'That's my job, for ever and ever.'

'Until the next adventure, then,' said Oberon.

'Until the next time,' agreed Gildevard, as he flexed his wings.

'Try to stay clear of buzzards, Gildevard,' barked Timber cheekily, as the eagle flew off, back to his cold and lonely mountain-top nest.

Timber was still a bit suspicious as to which of them was to blame – Gildevard or Bodric. There was no doubt that the buzzard had lied, but had the eagle told them everything? He had a nagging doubt.

Over on the pond, the two swan couples had made a grand entrance, returning with the ducks. Everyone was delighted, including the children. At last both the duck house and the swan house would be full. All the garden birds were in full summer song, and the bees were buzzing loudly with Operation Pollination well under way, this time under the command of the new Balthazar.

As expected, Timber and his best friend Teddy were elected the new leaders of the garden, to follow in the paw-steps of the Brigadier and Sylvie. The two old pets were happy to pass their duties to the younger pair.

With Worfeus dead, the forest was slowly coming back to life. The back field had returned to a bright lush green. The trees were standing tall and straight again as the sunshine broke through to the woodland floor. Some of the Grindlewood rabbits and birds had already returned to their natural homes in the woods. There were berries and mushrooms growing wild in amongst the recovering foliage. The forest would soon be a real forest again.

With school over for the summer, the children were looking forward to spending a lot of time together.

'What a super big dog he is!' said Luke, giving Timber a big hug. 'I can't wait to see him pull your sledge in the snow next winter! Can he really do it by himself?'

'He sure can. It's great fun. And Luke, Dougal is the super-dog, Timber is the *Super-mal*!' said Jamie, laughing.

'Super-dog! Super-mal!' the children chanted. Timber was chuffed, and Dougal was very pleased at being called a super-dog at last. Teddy was purring loudly. He was honoured to be Timber's best friend, and now he was his garden deputy too.

'You know, we're living in Grindlewood one whole year now,' said Jamie.

'And just think of all the amazing things we've discovered,' said Jemima.

'That the animals can talk,' said Jamie.

'Like all that magic,' said Jemima.

'And we know so many of Grindlewood's secrets now,' said Abigail. 'And I'll bet there are lots more.'

'Eh, like I'm alive and out of that statue!' said Luke, pointing to himself.

The four of them laughed.

'What do you think will be next?' said Abigail.

'Next?' said the boys together.

'There's a lot more in Abigail's books, you know, really there is. We're going to find lots more magic round here. I'm sure of it,' said Jemima, confidently.

'Me too,' said Abigail.

'Well, I'm ready for the next adventure,' said Jamie.

'If it's anything like the last time, we'll need to be ready,' said Luke.

'And we will be,' said Jamie, brandishing his wooden sword.

Timber barked.

'And we'll always have Timber with us too!' said Jamie.

The children could hear Jamie and Jemima's mum calling them, and reluctantly they left the fairy house. It was time for Luke and Abigail to go home. The summer holidays were going to be very exciting whenever these four friends got together.

Timber always did his final patrol of the day on his own. The other pets were already asleep, even Teddy.

'Woo-woo-woo! Woo-woo-woo!' he called to the night. 'I am Timber, and I am the protector of Grindlewood. Woo-woo, Woo-woo! Woo-woo, Woo-woo!' Satisfied that all was well, he returned to the kennel and curled up beside his friends.

Under the floorboards in the fairy house, Wanda's crystal key lay beside the other treasures in the little wooden box. It began to glow again. It twinkled and twitched and then it flipped over. It seemed to want to jump out of the box, eager to do something. Did it hold more ancient magic? Would it unlock the door to another adventure, or perhaps reveal more of Grindlewood's secrets?

Only the key could know. Only time would tell.

THE END

Acknowledgements

This book would not have been possible without so many wonderful people, all of whom deserve a special mention.

Heartfelt thanks once again to my marvellous editor, Robert Doran; to my wonderful illustrator, Fintan Taite; to Chenile Keogh for producing my book in all its many forms; to my extended family and close friends who continue to encourage and support my work; to my enthusiastic young readers who have road-tested this second instalment in the Grindlewood series and look forward to the next outing!

I owe a very special mention also to my husband, Angelo, for all his love and support and hard work. Without him, my stories may not have seen the light of day.

The Secrets of Grindlewood

BOOK 1 AVAILABLE NOW

Jamie and Jemima Grindle move to Grindlewood House with their pets Timber and Teddy. But they soon realise that all is not as it seems in their beautiful new garden. There is dark magic at work in the nearby forest.

The good witch Wanda has been defeated and now the wicked warlock Worfeus is plotting to destroy Grindlewood and its enchanted garden. Only Wanda's powerful spells, written on a secret scroll, can rid the world of the warlock.

Timber must lead the animals of Grindlewood in their quest to find the scroll and defeat their enemy. But where is the scroll hidden and will they find it before Worfeus? Is there really enough magic in their wild garden to help them defeat such evil?

"A classic tale to delight readers aged 8–12."

Sue Leonard, Author and Journalist

BOOK 3

The Secrets of Grindlewood

When she hears that the residents of Grindlewood garden have defeated the wicked warlock Worfeus, the Forest Queen decides to enlist their help to release her from the Worfagon's curse. But it soon becomes clear that the Queen is not the kind and gentle leader she once was.

After years of suffering under the Worfagon 'tree spell', the Queen is now bitter and angry. She is obsessed with Jamie's beautiful dog, Timber, and she threatens to keep him for herself unless the children agree to come to her aid. They must find the lost *Ancient Book of Magic*, which holds powerful spells that can free her.

Timber the brave malamute dog once again leads Jamie, Jemima and their loyal band of pets in a hair-raising adventure. Together they must face down mortal danger, dark magic and evil enemies to free the trapped Forest Queen and ensure Timber's safe return.

AVAILABLE IN 2015